A Home Subscription! It's the easiest and most convenient way to get every one of the exciting Coventry Romance Novels! . . .And you get 4 of them FREE!

You pay nothing extra for this convenience: there are no additional charges. . .you don't even pay for postage! Fill out and send us the handy coupon now, and we'll send you 4 exciting Coventry Romance novels absolutely FREE!

SEND NO MONEY, GET THESE
FOUR BOOKS FREE!

- -

C0582

MAIL THIS COUPON TODAY TO:
**COVENTRY HOME
SUBSCRIPTION SERVICE
6 COMMERCIAL STREET
HICKSVILLE, NEW YORK 11801**

YES, please start a Coventry Romance Home Subscription in my name, and send me FREE and without obligation to buy, my 4 Coventry Romances. If you do not hear from me after I have examined my 4 FREE books, please send me the 6 new Coventry Romances each month as soon as they come off the presses. I understand that I will be billed only $9.00 for all 6 books. There are no shipping and handling nor any other hidden charges. There is no minimum number of monthly purchases that I have to make. In fact, I can cancel my subscription at any time. The first 4 FREE books are mine to keep as a gift, even if I do not buy any additional books.

For added convenience, your monthly subscription may be charged automatically to your credit card.

☐ Master Charge   ☐ Visa
42101   **42101**

Credit Card #_____

Expiration Date_____

Name_____
                              (Please Print)
Address_____

City _____State _____Zip _____

Signature_____

☐ Bill Me Direct Each Month **40105**
Publisher reserves the right to substitute alternate FREE books. Sales tax collected where required by law. Offer valid for new members only. Allow 3-4 weeks for delivery. Prices subject to change without notice.

THE
Marriage Bargain

Rachelle Edwards

FAWCETT COVENTRY • NEW YORK

THE MARRIAGE BARGAIN

This book contains the complete text of the original hardcover
edition.

Published by Fawcett Coventry Books, CBS Educational and
Professional Publishing, a division of CBS Inc., by arrangement
with Robert Hale Limited

ISBN: 0-449-50288-0

Printed in the United States of America

First Fawcett Coventry printing: May 1982

10   9   8   7   6   5   4   3   2   1

THE
Marriage Bargain

One

"Valentina! Valentina!"

The bedroom door burst open and a young woman rushed in, her curls flying, her skirts held above her ankles.

Valentina Woodville struggled to sit up against the lace-edged pillows, looking both bewildered and alarmed.

"Daphne? Daphne, dear, whatever is amiss?"

"Mama, you goosecap," her sister replied, plumping down on the bed heavily, causing Valentina to wince. "Mama is in such a taking."

"When is she not?" the other girl retorted, casting her sister a wry smile.

"Have you forgotten what is happening today? Madame Furneaux will be here within the hour and you are not even out of bed yet."

Valentina's indulgent smile faded. "Why did you have to remind me of that, Daphne? I was just having such lovely thoughts."

"Of what?"

"Of whom," Valentina corrected in a mysterious tone.

"Oh, do tell me!"

Her sister's eyes sparkled with mischief. "Never you mind!"

Daphne tossed back her mane of curls, so similar in colour to the dark brown ones of her elder sister. "I'll warrant it is not Lord Stockdale who fills your thoughts. Your attitude is most amazing for someone who is to be wed by the end of the week."

Momentarily Valentina buried her head in her hands. "Oh, do not remind me! I keep hoping something will happen to prevent it going ahead."

"What could possibly happen now?"

"Lord Stockdale could cry off," Valentina suggested.

"Most unlikely," her sister retorted.

The prospective bride wrinkled her snub nose. "I know, but he could get the pox, I suppose."

At this suggestion, Daphne jumped to her feet. "Oh, you wicked creature!" When her sister exhibited no sign of contrition, Daphne went on, "Your reason is totally unhinged, Valentina. I only hope when I receive an offer of marriage it will be from someone as eligible as Lord Stockdale."

Her sister cast her a look of disgust. "Then I can only regret you have not yet come out, for I would gladly exchange places with you. It is not my attic which is to let, but Papa's for accepting Stockdale's offer when so many others wished me to be their bride."

"I shall not mind my sister being a marchioness."

"That is all very well but *you* do not have to marry that monster."

Daphne looked shocked again. "Has he ill-treated you?"

"You know he has been all kindness and solicitude."

"I had noticed," Daphne answered wryly

and then, glancing at a discarded breakfast tray, "You have scarce eaten anything."

"I am not hungry."

"Then you will not mind..." Daphne helped herself to a slice of bread and butter and then, glancing at the assortment of gifts lying on the counterpane, asked with her mouth full, "Surely they haven't *all* arrived this morning."

Valentina nodded happily and buried her nose in a posy of flowers. "This is from Lord Mayne. The marchpane is from Lord Livesey."

"I suppose all this will continue after you're married?"

"How can I possibly stop them?" Valentina asked, her eyes wide with innocence.

Daphne lowered her voice to a conspiratorial whisper. "Shall you take one as a gallant?"

"I wouldn't have to if I was to marry the man of my choice."

A maid arrived with water and Valentina threw back the bedcovers. Her sister stood to one side, reaching for a piece of cold toast as she did so.

"You mean Lord Mayne, I suppose." When Valentina did not answer, her sister went on in a thoughtful way, "I am bound to say Lord Stockdale is by far superior in every way."

Valentina had picked up her hair brush and was pulling it through a mass of tangled curls, to which powder still clung, when she threw it down on the dressing table.

"He is not to my taste and I cannot get anyone in this household to believe that. Mama says such modesty in a wife is to be prized and that Lord Stockdale must appreciate such diffidence. It is as though my entire family has taken leave of its senses. By the end of the week I shall be married to that man, and I can scarce bear the thought of it."

"That man is very rich and incredibly influential," her sister pointed out, still eating.

Valentina allowed her shift to be slipped over her head. "He is also quite ugly and old—thirty at the very least. Why, he is almost as old as Papa."

"Papa is not so old."

The other girl made a sound of annoyance. "Stockdale has only found favour because he is one of his cronies."

"They may be acquainted but I am certain they are not close friends. In any event, in my opinion he is not so ill favoured."

"How can he compare to Lord Mayne or Lord Livesey, or indeed to Hanson Pritchard, who are all most handsome?"

"There is more to a man than his outward appearance, and I must confess Lord Stockdale always dresses with taste. His face shows no sign of dissipation and he presents a fine figure. I am persuaded his coats are not padded and he shows a fine leg."

At such a pronouncement Valentina could not help but look amused. "La! How well you have studied him."

Daphne cast her sister a hurt look. "You would find fault with a fat goose. You must allow Papa to know what is best for you."

"How can I acknowledge that when he will see me wed to a man I loathe?"

Daphne was visibly taken aback, so much so she returned a piece of beef to the plate. "Those are exceedingly harsh words, Valentina."

Biting her lip, the other girl sank down on to a stool to be enveloped in a powdering robe. The maid and the younger Miss Woodville exchanged exasperated looks.

"I was merely indifferent to him before his offer was accepted, but I truly loathe him now."

"Then it will be in your own best interests to change your mind before Friday." Daphne said pertly before going to the window.

The maidservant giggled until Valentina's ferocious look silenced her.

Daphne began to jump up and down excitedly. "Madame Furneaux has arrived with the gowns, so you'd better hurry, Valentina." She went towards the door. "In the meantime I shall be glad to try on my gown."

Her sister turned in her seat, causing the comb to slip and her maid to gasp.

"Can you have words with Mama, Daphne? Make her see how desperately unhappy I am."

"It will make no odds, I fear. She declares every female is apprehensive of such a responsibility as marriage, especially when it is to a man of high rank. She is persuaded you will be happy enough once you are the Marchioness of Stockdale. You are more to be envied then pitied, Valentina," she added as she went out, leaving her sister glaring furiously into the dressing table mirror.

"If mam'selle will only stand still I will have the gown fitted in a trice," the dressmaker complained as she arranged the gown of white damask and silver lace about Valentina's slim form.

"I have no wish to prolong this matter," she replied in a dull voice.

"I have heard it said, mam'selle, that St. George's will never again see so beautiful a bride."

"Nor one so miserable," Valentina could not help but add.

Daphne cast her a reproachful look but the dressmaker only laughed as she continued to pin up the hem.

"La! How often I have heard those words from the lips of a prospective bride."

She had caught Valentina's attention now. "Truly?"

"Oh, do not encourage her, madame," Daphne implored.

"It is perfectly true, I assure you. I have heard similar laments from so many of my clients. But it is also true that within a six month, when they return to me for new gowns, they are radiant and quite reconciled to their new situation."

Valentina's momentary look of hope died. "I am not so capricious, madame."

The door opened and Lady Woodville brushed in, clasping her hands together when she caught sight of her daughter in her wedding finery. "Oh, how lovely you look! You are a vision, my dear. Is she not, Madame Furneaux?"

"The loveliest bride it has been my privilege to dress, my lady."

As Lady Woodville wiped away a surreptitious tear, her daughter said tartly, "Save the tears for Friday, Mama, when they will be more in keeping."

"Such nonsense, but you do look radiant. No wonder Stockdale is captivated by your charms."

"My portion more like," her daughter muttered darkly.

Lady Woodville affected not to hear and pecked her elder daughter on the cheek. "How are you this morning, my dear?"

Knowing that complaints were useless, she answered in a tone of resignation, "Tolerable, Mama."

"Did you sleep well? We must guard against dark shadows."

"Yes, Mama."

"This is, understandably, a great strain for all of us."

"I am the one to be married, Mama, and I'd as lief go to the guillotine with some of those poor Frenchies as stand up at the altar with Stockdale."

Lady Woodville threw up her hands in horror. "Oh, you wicked creature! To think I have nurtured a viper to my bosom."

"You do not know what you say, Mam'sell," Madame Furneaux informed her.

Daphne looked rueful and a moment later Lady Woodville said, her good spirits not dampened for long at such a time, "You are understandably overwrought by all the hurry-scurry. In a sen'night you will be at Stockdale and able to regain your spirits entirely."

As such an utterance was sufficient to cast her sister's spirits into a further decline, Daphne could not help but giggle.

"That is perfect, I think," the dressmaker declared, standing back to admire her own handiwork, "but do not, I beg of you, mam'selle, lose any more weight before Friday."

"I cannot eat. My appetite is entirely gone."

The dressmaker looked shocked. "You must eat! Your husband will not like you to be a bag of bones. Now, mam'selle, if you will be kind enough to step out of this gown and put on the blue silk, you will see how it becomes you."

With ill-grace Valentina did as she was asked. The blue satin exactly matched the colour of her eyes and complimented the creamy smoothness of a complexion which had been eulogised by so many *beaux* of the *ton* since her come out several months earlier. As Valentina reluctantly gazed at her own reflection, she was forced to acknowledge that she had never looked in better spirits and involuntarily tears pricked at her eyes.

As she hastened to struggle out of the gown, Lady Woodville turned on her heel. "Well, now I have seen that is satisfactorily resolved I must have words with Cook about the catering arrangements for the ball tomorrow..."

"Mama..."

She paused by the door. "Yes, dear?"

Clad only in her shift, Valentina took a step towards her mother. "Mama, can you not have words with Papa?"

The woman was wide-eyed, her ample bosom heaving with agitation. It was difficult for her children to believe she had been one of the great Society beauties of her day.

"About what, dearest?"

"Lord Stockdale," she answered, her humility and patience at a low ebb. "Can you not talk with him about this marriage?"

Lady Woodville shrugged and lifted a cologne-soaked handkerchief to her face. "But all the talking has been done, dear."

A footman knocked at the door and Lady Woodville took from him a card. After reading it she put one hand to her head, knocking her lace cap askew.

"Mama..."

"Oh, do not trouble me now! Lady Stockdale is here. She will not take kindly to being kept waiting. Do get dressed quickly, dear, so we can receive her with no further delay."

Valentina rocked backwards on her

heels at the news that her future mother-in-law was calling.

"What can she want?"

"To make acquaintance with her future daughter-in-law," Daphne pointed out.

"She is bound to take me in dislike. Is there no end to my torment?"

"She will only take you in dislike if you insist upon declaring how much you hate her son." Valentina cast her a dark look and then Daphne ventured "You may find her charming."

"I know her by repute. She is excessive proud, but I suppose I must go and be civil to her, although it will be difficult to do so knowing she has spawned that man."

Daphne began to leave the room and as her sister was being hooked into her gown, Valentina said, "Oh, you must come too, Daphne. I need your support."

Daphne's eyes sparkled with mischief. "Naturally I will come. I would not miss this meeting for anything!"

Two

The dowager marchioness of Stockdale was ushered into the large drawing room and the three ladies awaiting her sank into deep curtsies.

Lady Stockdale, although of slight build, nevertheless had an aura about her which induced subservience in all those who met her. Clad in brown velvet with a matching hat adorned by many feathers which added considerably to her height, she did present a formidable appearance.

"My lady, how honoured we are by your presence," Lady Woodville cried.

The other lady's response was somewhat cooller as she glanced around the room, peering at everyone and everything down a high-bridged nose which was remarkably similar to the one bestowed upon her son.

"I deemed it proper to call in on you before the ball tomorrow evening."

Her eyes darted around the room and came to rest on Valentina who stood with her hands clasped demurely in front of her and her eyes downcast in a suitably modest way.

Valentina was not happy with the woman's haughty attitude, nor her mother's, which she considered to be obsequious.

"Allow me to present to you my elder daughter, Valentina."

The girl raised her eyes at last to discover that her future mother-in-law was not regarding her with overt favour.

"Indeed. So this is the prospective bride. Well, you are as handsome as I recall."

She glanced at Daphne then and Lady Woodville said quickly, "This, Lady Stockdale, is my younger daughter not yet come out."

Lady Stockdale turned away and drew

in a sharp breath. "You are to be complimented on your family, Lady Woodville."

She walked across the room, and, blushing furiously, Lady Woodville followed her, saying, "Do be seated, my lady."

The dowager sat down on a sofa and removed her gloves. Daphne glanced worriedly at her sister as their mother indicated that they, too, should be seated, for her expression was one of silent mutiny and one that was likely to erupt at any moment.

"I am only just come to Town," Lady Stockdale announced as she folded her gloves carefully.

"I trust that your journey was a good one," her hostess ventured.

"Journeys to one of my age, Lady Woodville, are always tiresome and to be avoided when necessary."

"Oh, I entirely agree," and then, realising what she had said, Lady Woodville went on stammering, much to her daughter's amusement, "I mean...travelling is always the most tedious...even to the young..."

"However, even though the journey takes a toll on my health and there is so real a risk of being held up by some rascally tobyman, there was no chance of my crying off. I must be present at my son's wedding. Duty, duty is everything.

"Needless to say," the dowager went on, "there was a deal to do at Stockdale House before I left so that it is fit to receive my son and his bride. I am now to take up a dower residence at Colesfield. *Otium cum dignitate* is my family motto and I truly believe one must retire from all things with dignity."

She glanced at Valentina who tried not to allow her relief show. Having her mother-in-law in another county was at least a small blessing.

"I trust that matters pertaining to the wedding are well in hand."

"Everything is arranged, my lady."

The dowager glanced at Valentina again. "My son has remained a bachelor too long, I admit, but that is entirely due to my influence. Before he departed on the Grand Tour of his youth I impressed upon him the importance of choosing the correct wife. After all, my son has an elevated position to maintain. He cannot marry anyone."

"Oh, indeed not," Lady Woodville agreed, warming to the conversation now.

"My daughter is very much aware of the honour of becoming Lady Stockdale."

"He has always been aware that he must marry a girl of high birth, and even though it would be pleasant for her to be sweet-natured, too, that is not of the greatest import. The Marchioness of Stockdale must know how to be a good—no—a great hostess. As a daughter of the Duke of Nantwich I was schooled early in my life in the art of entertaining."

Outwardly Valentina remained demure but inwardly she was seething, something of which her sister was very much aware.

"Oh indeed, 'tis of the greatest import," Lady Woodville agreed. "My daughter, I am certain, will not fail in her duties in all areas of her marriage."

Lady Stockdale looked not the least reassured, but she addressed Valentina at last. "I shall pray, my dear Miss Woodville, that your nursery will always be full."

Valentina sat up even more straight and her sister took in a sharp breath. She even raised her hand slightly in an attempt to avert a sharp retort.

"Yours was not, my lady."

Startled, the dowager did not immediately answer. Lady Woodville began to say something but Lady Stockdale held up her hand.

"Your daughter, plain-spoken as she may be, has uttered nothing but the truth." She fixed Valentina with a steely eye. "Alexander is my only child and that is the greatest tragedy of my life."

Contrite at last, Valentina lowered her eyes.

"Would you take a dish of tea with us, Lady Stockdale?" Lady Woodville invited, eager to change the direction of the conversation.

The dowager got to her feet. "No, I thank you. This meeting must be a brief one. As I visit Town rarely I needs must call on several old acquaintances."

She glanced at Valentina and inclined her head. "Until tomorrow, Miss Woodville."

Lady Woodville hurried after her as the girls dutifully curtsied again. When the door closed on the two women Valentina gave vent to her annoyance at last with a series of screams.

"Having the vapours will not help anything," Daphne pointed out.

"It helps me," her sister retorted. "Oh, she is as insufferable as I had supposed."

"You are not marrying Lady Stockdale," Daphne pointed out.

"He is no better than she. Pride and arrogance; he inherited them from her."

"She *is* the daughter of a duke."

Daphne went to the window and when she looked out a slow smile crossed her lips.

"Here is something to cast out your megrims."

Eager for any diversion Valentina hurried to join her sister at the window. "What is so miraculous about Harry's curricle? He will only tease me as you do."

Daphne grinned. "Lord Mayne arrived with our brother."

Valentina's countenance immediately brightened and she ran to a mirror to ascertain that her appearance was at its very best. Her sister began to laugh and Valentina cast her a curious look as she patted a renegade curl into place.

"May I join in the funning, Daphne?"

"I was just recalling your face when Lady Stockdale mentioned the nursery."

"Do not remind me! It was all I could do not to explode with anger."

"Is Stockdale's name really Alexander?"

"I believe so. I have never taken much note of it."

Daphne considered it for a moment or two before musing, "It is quite a nice name."

"No, it is not. It is disagreeable like the man himself."

Daphne shook her head wryly and moments later Mr. Harry Woodville and Viscount Mayne were announced.

At the sight of her love Valentina's heart began to thump noisily and in a futile attempt to stop it she pressed a hand to her breast.

The fair-haired young man smiled as his eyes came to rest on her.

"Miss Woodville, how good it is to see you," he said, pressing his lips to her hand.

Her cheeks grew pink. "We did not look to see you today, Lord Mayne."

"Your brother and I rode in the Park this afternoon and when you did not appear I prevailed upon Harry to bring me here lest you were afflicted with some indisposition."

Valentina's smile faded despite her

pleasure at seeing him and she turned away to hide her anguish. "I am to be wed on Friday and there is a deal to be done in the meantime."

He frowned and lowered his voice to a whisper. "No one is more aware of it than I, Miss Woodville. I am the most wretched of men. I cannot conceive what I have done to deserve this torment. If only Sir Arthur had considered my suit favourably."

Suddenly her demeanour brightened. "I will appeal to him. I am quite persuaded he has no notion how I really feel and he cannot fail to heed my unhappiness."

Lord Mayne looked startled. "But 'tis only three days before you wed Stockdale."

"Exactly," she answered with a smile. "I am not wed yet."

"Papa, may I have words with you?"

Valentina was leaning over the baluster rail and her father glanced up at her as he strode across the hall.

His face broke into a smile at the sight of his elder daughter. "Is it of import, my dear?"

"Yes."

He glanced at his pocket watch. "Very

well, but five minutes only for I am due at White's."

She came quickly down the stairs. "I will detain you for only a short while."

She went with him into the library, as anxious as he not to waste time.

"Now," he said pouring a glass of claret. "What is it? A shortage of pin money, eh?"

Valentina smiled faintly. "No. You have been very generous."

He gave her a coy grin. "Well, not long now, m'dear, before my little girl becomes the Marchioness of Stockdale."

She paused to lace her fingers together before saying, "That is what I wish to talk about. Are you aware, Papa, that I do not wish to marry Lord Stockdale?"

Sir Arthur's eyes opened wide and the claret spilled on to the tray as he put down his glass. "Good grief! You cannot wish to cry off!"

"You've known all the time how I felt about him."

"What nonsense! An admirable fellow. Excellent match, Stockdale."

"I don't love him."

"Love!" He began to laugh. "You don't

know the fellow yet, but you will love him, m'dear. Of course you will."

"I won't, Papa," she answered, becoming impatient again.

Sir Arthur's face had a tendency to turn red and it did so now. "What's this? Disobedience? Let me tell you m'father arranged *my* marriage and that hasn't turned out so bad."

"Life is different now, Papa. Many people marry for love."

"Ridiculous! There are far more important matters to consider. What a pretty pass! Paupers and commoners can marry for love, not the likes of us, Valentina."

"Lord Mayne is not a commoner."

"Ah, so that's the way it is. One of Harry's rackety friends. He has no face of his own. Lives on his aunt's largess. Do you wish to marry a basket scrambler?"

"Yes," she answered unequivocally. "We could live well on my portion alone."

"You would receive nothing in return."

"Happiness, Papa," she told him quietly and his face became even redder.

"You're just a moon-struck child. You'll be over that quickly enough and then what, eh? He's no fit match for you. Stockdale, on the other hand, is a fine fellow."

"He's a rake, a deep gambler and a drunkard."

Sir Arthur laughed again. "So are many admirable men and it makes no odds. Do you think Mayne is a saint?"

"No, Papa, but at least I love him."

"Oh, this is nothing but pre-nuptial vapours. Only think," he added slyly, "you'll be the Marchioness of Stockdale. Many a chit would be in high snuff at the prospect."

"Oh, Papa, it is no use your trying to humour me. I will be cast into the dismals for ever if I marry Stockdale."

Her father drained his glass. "Enough of this tarradiddle, girl. The contracts have been signed. 'Tis all arranged and I cannot allow you to cry off even if I was in a mind to do so, which I assure you I am not."

Her eyes clouded with tears. "Am I to have no say in this matter?"

"You are too young to decide your own future. It is for those who are wiser to do so for you. Let us hear no more about crying off. Is that understood?"

"Yes, Papa," she answered with a

meekness which was rare for her. "I am sorry to have troubled you."

Daphne was waiting in her sister's room when she arrived back looking disconsolate.

"He would not listen," she said the moment she saw her sister's woeful expression.

Valentina sighed profoundly. "To Papa, Stockdale is a paragon of all virtues," she replied, sinking down on to her day bed.

"Even I know he is not that. However, I do suspect that many of your acquaintances would feel quite differently about him and it has little to do with his wealth or his situation."

"Oh, I have no doubt many foolish females will continue to pursue Stockdale. Heaven knows I have never been one of them, and marriage to me will not divert him from the type of creature with whom he consorts at present. What is more, that suits me very well."

Daphne cast her sister a worried look then. "You...would not do...anything foolish, would you?"

Valentina looked up at her. "What would you suggest?"

"Elopement?"

Her sister smiled. "I am not such a goose. No," she added with a sigh, "I have exhausted all possibility of not marrying him now. There is no honourable way of crying off. I shall be tied to Stockdale until one of us dies."

Daphne drew back. "Valentina! You cannot...you do not..."

"Chucklehead," her sister scoffed. "I mean that as a dutiful daughter I shall marry Stockdale as arranged."

"Oh, how you relieve me! I have been so concerned for you."

"Save your satisfaction, Daphne," Valentina answered darkly. "My parents have sacrificed me to their own ambition and when I pine away and die they will regret it most sorely. Indeed they will," she added, relishing the picture she had, herself, conjured up.

Three

The ball to be held at Woodville House prior to Valentina's wedding to the Marquis of Stockdale was to be eagerly attended. The marriage, culminating as it did Valentina's first social season, was the talk of the town. As an accredited beauty and a considerable heiress, her betrothal to so eligible a bachelor as the Marquis of Stockdale was a great talking point amongst all their acquaintances. Before the main body of guests arrived, the streets around the Woodville town house were already choked with carriages as those closest to the two families were invited to a banquet which preceded the ball itself.

Despite her final acceptance of her situation, Valentina had to be summoned from her room when the dinner hour approached. The servant sent to fetch her discovered Valentina staring at her own magnificence in the cheval mirror, as motionless as a statue.

The rest of her family, who were already assembled at the head of the curving staircase, turned as she approached.

"Oh, do hurry, my dear," Lady Woodville urged, "Lord Stockdale's carriage is pulling into the drive and it wouldn't do for you of all people to be absent."

"By jove!" Harry exclaimed. "Can this really be *my* sister? You look every bit the marchioness already."

She gave him a faint smile and Daphne said, "You do look quite wonderful, Valentina."

"Naturally," she replied. "Would not any bride be radiant on the eve of her wedding?"

The blue gown was exquisite, appliqued with semiprecious stones. Her hair was curled high and adorned by jewelled pins sent by the dowager marchioness. Around her throat nestled a fall of diamonds and sapphires sent to her as a wedding gift by the marquis. They were fabulous by any standards and sight of them that afternoon had given Lady Woodville a fit of the vapours so severe that her maid had been obliged to burn feathers. Needless to say, the recipient had not been moved by her husband-to-be's generosity.

"My dear, once you are married all manner of fabulous jewels will be yours," Lady Woodville whispered.

"You know very well I want none of them."

Her mother pinched her arm. "You are an ungrateful hussy. I only pray that your sister makes half such a match as this."

Valentina fell silent, knowing her more obedient sister would never gainsay her parents' choice of a husband. The realisation gave her a guilty start, reminding her of her own fortunate situation about which she could not rejoice.

As the marquis and dowager marchioness were announced, Valentina clasped her hands tightly together, aware that her palms were damp. Lady Stockdale wore a magnificent, but outmoded, gown of purple velvet, although her jewels were very fine.

As they paused at the foot of the stairs, the marquis looked up. He was not much taller than Valentina herself, something she noted constantly with little pleasure. When he addressed her she was obliged to look directly at him whereas when spoken to by Lord Mayne, or one of her other *beaux*, she found herself in the delectable position of having to gaze up at them.

However, Lord Stockdale was sartorially elegant, wearing a plain, dark evening coat with gold buttons. And there was a diamond the size of an egg pinned to the lace of his neckcloth. As most fashionable men preferred, since the Revolution in France, he wore his natural hair cut short with curls which framed his face. Only older men and Macaronis, of whom a few were present, retained the use of wigs.

Although Valentina could find no fault with his appearance, nevertheless it did not please her. When his dark eyes met hers she stared back at him impassively, for the sight of this man moved her only to anger. She was only relieved that he did not embarrass her with overt displays of affection.

Secretly, she was convinced he felt no more for her than she did for him, and this only increased her opposition to his suit. The thought of being married to a man who wished only for a rich bride to mother an heir to his titles and host his soirées, merely served to increase her ire.

As he escorted his mother up the staircase, Lady Stockdale surveyed them all through her quizzing glass.

"You look very fine," she conceded to Valentina as she allowed the glass to drop.

The recipient of the compliment gave her an acid smile. "I am so glad you approve, my lady."

The smile faded somewhat as Lord Stockdale took her hand and raised it formally to his lips.

"You look so dazzling you contrive to make the jewels look dull."

"I shall always be at pains to be a credit to you, my lord."

Her mother cast her a look of profound relief.

"I have never doubted it," the marquis replied and then adding, when she would have turned away. "I believe I am the most envied man in Town."

"And I, so I am told, the most envied woman." She smiled again. "I wonder if it will always be so, Lord Stockdale."

He frowned and she flipped open her fan, turning away as the first of their guests began to stream up the stairs.

During the entire time she had known the marquis they had never been alone together, which suited Valentina very well. Their conversations had been those of polite strangers, but now, for the first time, she began to realise they would soon be spending a great deal of time together. It was a thought she had always put to the back of her mind, but the time was fast approaching when she would no longer be able to do so.

In all their dealings she had been cool and polite and no more was expected of her, but soon that must change; her dislike of him would be all too apparent.

As the guests came up the stairs in a seemingly never ending stream, once again she put all thoughts of her impending marriage from her mind. When she glanced back at her future husband he was still casting her a curious look and, feeling sick at heart, she forced a welcoming smile to her lips as her friends, relatives and acquaintances clamoured to wish her happy.

"My country dance, Miss Woodville."

Valentina swung round on her heel to come face to face with Lord Mayne. Her cheeks were already pink due to the amount of champagne she had drunk and the fact that she had not been obliged to sit out one set. By contrast he looked pale and tense.

"Yes, indeed," she answered breathlessly and allowed him to lead her into the dance, her head held proudly.

As they took their place in the set she stole a glance at him as he faced her, tall and proud.

"Your parents must be very proud of you tonight," he said at last.

"Oh, indeed," she answered wryly, "and of themselves. Next Season the circus will begin again when my sister has her come out."

"They will be hoping for as good a match for her."

"A man with a fortune of his own and a title—no doubt you are correct, but I pray my sister will marry the man of her choice whoever he may be."

As she spoke, she caught sight of Lord Stockdale who had also joined the set. The lady with him seemed delighted to be his partner as her frequent laughter proved. When the marquis caught sight of Valentina he cast her a slight smile which she affected not to see, returning her attention to Lord Mayne.

"I shall not be at St George's on Friday," he declared. "It would be more than I could bear to see you exchange vows with that man."

"That is a great relief to me, for I could not bear to know you were there."

The music started up and as they began to dance Lord Mayne said in a harsh whisper, "Sir Arthur made the correct decision." When Valentina cast him a startled look he went on, "I could not give you the station you deserve, my dear Miss Woodville. When I caught sight of you tonight I realised it was so. You were made to be magnificently bejewelled and gowned and to receive the approbation of your peers."

She gave him a look of scorn. "Please, I beg of you do not join in the general chorus. Do you truly believe I care a fig for the jewels and title?"

"Not now, perhaps, but one day you will. Even though I cannot provide what you truly deserve, I am glad for your sake that you go to a man who can."

"It seems everyone is delighted save me," she answered tartly.

"It is useless for us to continue torturing ourselves, Miss Woodville. Cannot you see that? We must put the past in its proper place. 'Tis the future which matters."

"Mine seems bleak."

"Perhaps not entirely."

The country dance ended. Lord Mayne bowed and Valentina curtseyed. "What do you mean?"

"Marriage is not the end of everything. Indeed, it can give you greater freedom than you enjoy at present."

She gazed at him curiously as crowds milled around them, but she was oblivious to everything except this man.

"Lord Stockdale is not the man to remain...constant, Miss Woodville," he continued. "Once there is a child in the nursery you might well be free to pursue your own fancies."

She stared at him in astonishment although she knew what he suggested was true for many couples.

"Is that what you wish for us, Lord Mayne?" she asked in a quiet voice.

He smiled at last. "No, I do not. I wish to share every aspect of your life, but that is not to be, so we needs must seek an alternative route to happiness. There is not much else and it would be better than nothing."

Valentina looked downcast. "Oh, that is not what I had in mind for us," she answered at last, looking away.

"It might well be all we can have."

As someone approached to claim her for the next set, Lord Mayne excused himself. She watched him go, her heart aching, her mind fatigued. However, at the sound of a voice at her ear she turned and smiled at the gentleman, responding to his charm in a way which belied the pain inside her.

The dowager Lady Stockdale watched the proceedings from a seat at the side of the dance floor. Sitting bolt upright in the high backed chair, every now and again she raised her quizzing glass to inspect the dancers. When she espied her son in the doorway of the ballroom she beckoned him to approach.

He bowed slightly before her and she patted the seat at her side.

"May I fetch you some refreshment, Mama?"

"No, I thank you, dear, but do sit by me a while unless you are engaged to dance."

"Not for the moment."

When he was seated she said, "Sir Arthur and Lady Woodville have done us proud, I feel."

"That is generally the opinion."

She raised her glass once more. "Your bride-to-be enjoys herself. She has scarce stopped dancing all evening."

"Miss Woodville is always energetic, Mama."

"However, I have not seen her stand up with you since you opened the dancing an hour ago."

He smiled faintly and gazed across the room to where Valentina was holding court.

"Only see the callow youths who flock around her. They are almost all of them unsuccessful suitors. Surely you do not object to my charity in allowing them to enjoy the delight which will be mine alone after Friday."

She cast him an ironic look. "For a prospective bridegroom you are exceeding generous. 'Tis most unlike you, Alexander."

"You surely do not expect me to behave like a mooncalf, Mama," he chided gently.

"Certainly not! Such foolish behaviour is for others."

He glanced across the room again. "Miss Woodville will make an admirable wife, a woman of high breeding and great fortune."

"But a trifle flighty, I fear."

"'Tis no more than youthful spirits, Mama. I guarantee that by the beginning of next Season she will be a responsible matron."

The dowager looked far from convinced. "I trust your judgement is correct."

"Is it not always?"

She gave him one of her rare smiles. "I own that it is." Then she frowned. "I have been quizzing her all evening."

"That is sufficient to give her an attack of the vapours," he teased and she responded by tapping him playfully on the arm.

"You must not jest about so serious a matter, my boy."

"I assure you I regard the matter of matrimony with the utmost seriousness."

The dowager raised her quizzing glass again and regarded Valentina through it. "She is like a young thoroughbred, full of high spirits, but as we all know thoroughbreds can be dangerous to those who would try to tame them."

"Oh, Mama," he answered wryly, taking his snuff box from his pocket and flicking open the lid, "I do not tame my horses; I break them to my will."

His mother gave a great barking laugh. "Indeed you do, my boy. Yes, indeed you do."

When he had put away his snuff box he glanced briefly at his pocket watch. "Supper will be served shortly. Do you have an arm?"

"Sir Arthur Woodville no less. Run along if you wish to take your bride-to-be into supper."

He found Valentina surrounded by admirers. When he approached they made way for him and her smile faded when she saw him.

"I have come to take you into supper, my dear."

"Lord Livesey has already bespoken the honour."

The marquis smiled at the young man. "I am certain Lord Livesey will be gracious enough to release you from the obligation."

Before the young man in question could answer, Lord Stockdale had taken Valentina's arm and was leading her towards the supper room. She began to protest and then thought better of it, hiding her furious face behind her fluttering fan instead.

"So many broken-hearted young men," the marquis murmured, smiling at her in a way which most ladies found devastating. It did not move Valentina, except to anger.

"And a similar complement of ladies," she responded.

"You flatter me, my dear."

She gave him an acid smile. "I did not mean to, I assure you. After all, there are many reasons for seeking an alliance other than admiration. Position, wealth are above a mere liking, are they not?"

The marquis seemed unaware of her sarcasm and he merely answered urbanely, "I am so glad you are aware of that, my dear."

The supper table was almost groaning

beneath the multitude of dishes. Valentina turned away from the marquis to hide her chagrin.

"It appears that no one will go hungry this night," he murmured as he surveyed the dishes.

He glanced at Valentina. "What shall you have, my dear? Lobster, beef, a little lamb mayhap?"

"I am not hungry."

He seemed taken aback. "You must be. Just a little. You have been so active this evening."

"I really could not eat for the excitement," she reiterated affecting languor.

He moved away from the table. "Then you must allow me to find you a seat, Miss Woodville. I shall then bring you a selection which is certain to tempt your appetite."

She gave him a look of pure contempt. "It will be to no avail, my lord."

The indulgent look faded from his face. "You really must learn to be more indulgent of my wishes," he said in a mild and yet resolute tone, which caused her more fear than anger. "If you do not eat you will grow thin and that is not becoming."

"It is a family failing and I doubt if anything can be done about it."

"The good country air and food at Stockdale will soon remedy that." He bowed stiffly and she noted that his dark eyes held a cold expression. "By your leave, ma'am."

Her eyes narrowed as she watched him approach the supper table. Her fan snapped shut and she swallowed a cry of vexation. The man was totally infuriating and she couldn't understand why no one else was aware of it. However, within a very few moments she was once again surrounded by friends and admirers to divert her angry thoughts.

"I cannot conceive why you are so calm," one young lady declared admiringly.

Valentina stared implacably at her fiancé's back, hoping that her hatred of him would, somehow, inflict some mischief.

"I am screaming inwardly," she replied, returning her attention to her friend who laughed, believing her to be merely witty. "In fact," she went on, warming to her own tragedy, "I am just like a captive bird beating its wings against the sides of a cage."

The marquis, who was deciding which dishes to sample, turned to look at her and involuntarily frowned. A lady standing next to the marquis at the supper table cast Valentina a glance, too, before she confided:

"Miss Woodville has a deal of charm, Lord Stockdale."

He gave the lady an urbane smile which couldn't fail to please before answering in a delighted tone, "Yes, ma'am, so I am told."

However, clearly he was not delighted when Valentina refused the food he had painstakingly chosen and brought to her.

"I did tell you I wished for nothing."

"You used to eat heartily," one young man pointed out.

"Miss Woodville eats with the delicacy of a bird," declared one of her admirers.

"An exotic bird with the most magnificent plumage," added another which caused Valentina's cheeks to turn pink.

"Honoria Seaton eats like a sow," giggled one young girl. "It is most unbecoming."

This statement made Valentina laugh for the first time. "Then she should marry a pig."

Although she hadn't meant to do so, she could not help but glance at her husband-to-be. His colour heightened slightly but apart from the fury she saw leap into his eyes he gave no outward show of anger.

"If I cannot persuade you to eat, I shall leave you to your friends." She sighed, almost with relief, but then he went on, "I must not monopolise you tonight, my dear. After all, once we are wed we shall have all the time in the world to be entirely alone together."

He nodded curtly and then turned on his heel. Valentina suddenly felt chill and involuntarily she shivered at the reminder which no amount of company could dispell.

Four

Lights from the staging inn glowed out of the darkness.

Lord Stockdale moved the curtain to one side of the carriage window, peered out and then said to his wife, "We are approaching the *Wayfarer* at last."

Valentina, sitting opposite to him in the opulently appointed travelling carriage, did not reply. Wrapped in a green velvet travelling cloak lined with ermine and a matching feathered hat, she had spent the two hours of their journey from London in silence with her face averted for fear he should wish to engage her in conversation.

He leaned forward slightly. "You will be glad of the chance to rest, for I am persuaded the events of today have overtaxed your strength, my dear."

"A little," she replied, glad of the lie.

He smiled faintly in the darkness. "Getting leg-shackled is an onerous business, I own."

The carriage was pulling into the inn courtyard and he added, "I am well-known at this particular hostelry. I stay here every time I travel to Stockdale. It is clean, the food excellent, and we shall be exceeding comfortable."

The carriage ground to a halt. Feet could be heard clattering on the cobbles as ostlers and post boys came running to take charge of the horses.

The carriage door swung open and the landlord was bowing low in front of them. Lord Stockdale climbed down as soon as the steps were lowered and immediately gave his hand to Valentina, who hesitated only momentarily before following him.

He released her hand immediately and despite her reluctance to be alone with him at last she was glad of the opportunity to stretch her legs. Despite the luxury of the

carriage, the road had been shockingly uneven, shaking them at every turn. Valentina ached in every bone in her body.

"Welcome, welcome, my lord," the landlord was saying, still bowing low as he followed them inside. "And you, my lady. Very
many welcomes. Everything is ready in ac-
cordance with your instructions, my lord."

Valentina gave him a faint smile and
went into the inn where a delicious smell
of food was emanating from the direction of
the kitchen. Despite herself Valentina felt
her appetite stirring.

The marquis followed her and behind
him came an army of servants, both his own
and those from the inn.

"You will wish to refresh yourself," he
said once they were inside.

"Yes, I would like that," she murmured,
keeping her eyes downcast. Her heart was
beating fast now with apprehension.

But then, much to her relief, he added,
"I shall await you downstairs."

She hurried up the stairs, her way
lighted by a branch of candles held by a
maidservant who eyed her with too much
boldness for her liking. Valentina was glad,

however, to be away from her husband, even though the respite must only be a short one.

Mary was waiting in the well-appointed bedchamber. Hot water was already in a bowl on the washstand. Mary took her mistress's cloak and hat, watching her anxiously all the while.

"It was a comfortable journey," the maid ventured at last, not quite certain of her mistress's mood.

"Yes, it was," Valentina answered with a sigh.

Dominating the room was a large four-poster bed and after walking over to it she deliberately turned away.

"I am told we shall be in Stockdale by noon tomorrow." Mary continued to watch her mistress anxiously, adding, "The sheets are clean and aired, the water's hot. You need have no fear on that score, for 'tis quite plain to me his lordship always has the best, ma'am, and that's something to be grateful for, if I may be permitted to say so."

"No you are not," Valentina scolded. "Don't lecture me on that score, Mary. 'Tis enough the *haut monde* believe me the most fortunate creature on earth."

The maid looked downcast. "I do beg your pardon, ma'am."

Valentina sighed again. "That's all right, Mary. If I am in high dudgeon it has nothing to do with you." She sat down at the dressing table, and surveyed her own reflection, turning her head first one way and then the other. "Tidy my hair, Mary, and then I must join his lordship downstairs. There seems no point in delaying for I am obliged to take up my obligations immediately."

The marquis was waiting for her in the private parlour where their dinner was to be served.

"Why, you look as rested as if you've just risen from your bed," he told her, raising her hand to his lips.

"Thank you," she murmured, feeling shy now.

Her mood was in no way helped by the knowledge of how she would have felt if this was a man she loved. However, she was determined not to give in to her inner feelings and she held up her head proudly.

"Shall we dine now?" he asked, as several servants began to bring in dishes.

"I am not very hungry," she told him as they were seated at the table.

He frowned. "Is this habitual, or is it because you have today become the Marchioness of Stockdale?" When she did not answer he signalled the servants to retire, saying, "I am persuaded you will regain your appetite in the country. I shall ensure that you do."

She watched as he heaped a selection of food on to his plate and when he offered it to her she shook her head. Despite this he placed it in front of her and began to fill another plate for himself.

"You must eat, even if it is only to please me. You must always endeavour to please me."

She could not look at him. It was infinitely easier to pick up her fork and eat.

"The wine is excellent," he said as he raised his glass. After gazing at her for what seemed to be a long time he added, "Let me drink a toast to you, my dear. To the new Marchioness of Stockdale."

He took a long drink and she could not help but say, "It seems a dozen toasts have been drunk this day."

"To us, Valentina, to us. I drink to you."

A moment later he went on, "Old Scratchit keeps a good cellar. Quite exceptional for a coaching inn."

"This is an excellent place by any standards," she was forced to concede. "It is most fortunate, for one hears so many stories of inferior holstelries."

"Over the years Scratchit has become accustomed to the likes of me and my friends and, of course," he added, "only the best is good enough for your first night as the Marchioness of Stockdale."

Her cheeks grew red at the reminder and he went on as he partook of the hearty meal and plentiful wine, "I'm persuaded you will like my country house. The air is good in Hertfordshire. It's fine riding country, too, and I know you have a good seat." He glanced at her as she picked at the food. "This is the first year no house party will be held there."

She gave him an earnest look then. "I would not object to it."

He smiled. "How generous you are on our honeymonth, my dear, but to me it is of far more import for us to become acquainted at last. We have scarce had an opportunity before now."

Valentina could not help but shudder and noting it her husband said as he meticulously wiped his hands and lips on a clean napkin, "You are cold. Even the best of inns are draughty places. Come to the fire and warm yourself a while."

He got up and as Valentina did so, too, she said, "Mayhap I had best retire, my lord. It has been a long day."

She almost held her breath as he gazed at her consideringly for a moment or two. Then he said, "Soon. Just sit with me a while. I would have words with you before we retire."

Not knowing whether to be glad or sorry she averted her eyes. "As you wish."

When she sat down on a settle near the fire the marquis paused to pour himself another glass of wine before crossing the room. Instead of sitting beside her as she feared he might, he remained standing and although she kept her head averted she knew he was watching her and his gaze was a disturbing one.

"This marriage is not very much to your fancy," he said after a lengthy silence.

Her heart sank for she had tried very hard not to let her feelings show, knowing it would be to her own disadvantage. But she had failed.

When she didn't answer he said in a harsher voice, "Look at me, Valentina."

Startled, she still averted her eyes and he reached forward, cupping her chin in his hand and forcing her to look at him. Her eyes were wide with fear and tears sparkled on her lashes.

"I...am...so...sorry," she stammered and he let her go, drawing back again, much to her relief. "I did not truly wish it to show."

His eyes were dark with a passion which frightened her, but his cool manner was at odds with that.

"Tell me what is it you dislike about me most?"

"No...thing. Truly, it is not that."

He sighed and put his empty glass on the mantel. "Then you must fancy yourself in love with another."

"It makes no odds now," she answered in a weary voice. "We are wed and I shall endeavour to become the wife you desire."

His lips twisted into the travesty of a smile in the flickering candlelight. "How noble of you, my dear."

He went across the room to fetch the

bottle of wine and then refilled his glass to the brim.

"If you knew how I felt why did you marry me?" she couldn't help but ask, her voice edged with bitterness and resentment.

He raised the glass to his lips and all but drained it at once. "As you said to me only the other evening, there are many reasons for marriage. Besides, when Sir Arthur accepted my offer I assumed you were also in agreement with his decision. By the time I realised you were not it was too late to cry off."

"I wish you did not know. You must believe that." She wrung her hands together in an unconscious gesture of despair. "Oh, it is wrong that marriages should be arranged in this way."

"It has always been done."

"But it must change."

"The world is fast changing. Our customs might do so, too, in time. Only see what is happening in France."

She shuddered at the thought and he went on, "This conversation is only a waste of time. A post mortem never helped a dead man. We must think of our future—yours and mine."

She shuddered again. "Tell me what you want of me."

"I have a proposition to make to you."

She looked up at him, fearful again. He was staring ahead, his hands clasped behind his back.

"This marriage is going to have little attraction for either of us, 'tis plain, so I deem it prudent, in view of that, to arrange for us to have a divorce."

Valentina's eyes grew wide. This was the last thing she had expected to hear from him.

"Lord Stockdale!"

He looked at her then, expressionlessly. "Does the prospect not appeal to you?"

"Yes, but...do you not realise what is involved? 'Tis no small step."

"An act of Parliament no less. Oh yes, my dear Valentina, I do understand exactly what is involved and it is not something to be done lightly, but I have a position of influence, a member of the House of Lords. Moreover I can afford to pay for the necessary legislation. It can be done with little scandal involved if we are prudent, and then we shall be free, you to follow your heart and I to find a more willing wife."

"That will not be difficult for you," she answered, eager to encourage him.

"Then I have been singularly unfortunate on this occasion."

The irony in his voice was lost on her for she still could scarce believe her ears. Despairingly she had visualised a life tied to this man who had displayed only the smallest degree of cordiality towards her.

Eagerly now she urged, "Only tell me what we are to do!"

He smiled then and she noted it transformed his demeanour from its severity to something far more likeable, but then her mood was a bland one now.

"Such eagerness, my dear. The notion evidently finds favour with you."

"You know it must."

"Not so hasty, my dear. Nothing is without its obligations and you have not yet heard what the price will be."

Her eager smile faded and she looked away. "How foolish of me to think it would be simple."

"You and I must enter into a bargain, Valentina."

Her lips twisted into a travesty of a

smile. "A Devil's bargain. Do I sell my soul to you, Lord Stockdale?"

At this he threw back his head and laughed. "Nothing so dramatic, I fear. What I propose is that, as planned, we ajourn to my estate for the summer, not on our honey-month, naturally."

She looked up at him, her eyes narrowed. "We are not to live as husband and wife?"

"Do you prefer that we should?"

She looked away quickly as he began to laugh again. She realised then that he had drunk almost the entire bottle of wine.

"You need have no fears on that score, my dear. When the Season begins we will return to London where you will take up residence in my house and appear to the world as the perfect wife and hostess. If, after the Season, you have acted the role I ask of you I will then put in motion the machinery of divorce. No blame will be attached to you."

He turned away to refill his glass and she stared at him in astonishment. "Lord Stockdale, I don't understand. Why do you wish me to do this?"

"Pride, my dear Valentina. To save

your husband's wretched pride." He looked at her once more, his face an expressionless mask. "Do I have your agreement?"

"I have no choice."

"You will be a good, loyal and obedient wife?"

"Yes," she hissed.

"Needless to say, this must remain our secret, and I shall expect not a breath of scandal to reach my ears about you in the coming months."

"I shall be most abstemious in all things, you may be certain."

"I hope so, because I insist upon it as a condition."

She looked up at him anxiously. "You will keep your word though, when the time comes?"

Clutching at the glass, he replied, "My dear, if you were a man I would call you out for that slight on my honour. You have the word of a gentleman." He put down the glass. "You must be greatly fatigued after all that has happened today. I will show you to your bedchamber."

Valentina hardly dared to think of what he had said. It seemed as though a miracle had happened.

She went slowly up the stairs, her way lighted by a branch of candles held aloft by the marquis. At the top of the stairs she scarce knew how to address him.

He raised her hand to his lips, saying, "Good night, my lady. Sweet dreams."

She curtseyed. "Good night, Lord Stockdale."

Thankfully she closed the door behind her, falling back against it and letting out a great sigh of relief. Her heart, heavy for so many weeks, was so light she wanted to sing and dance. She would do as he asked, for the reward of freedom must be worth all the effort involved.

Mary had been dozing by the fire, but as the door clicked shut she jumped to her feet.

"Oh, my lady, I have your nightgown warming. Only let me help you into it quickly. Lord Stockdale will be impatient to join you."

Valentina did not gainsay the woman and she had completed her mistress's toilette very quickly. She saw Valentina to her bed and, giving a quick curtsey, she hurried away to her own rest.

By this time Valentina could scarce

contain her glee. She clutched the pillow next to hers close to her, laughing as she did so and jumping up and down on the mattress with sheer and unadulterated joy.

Five

"That bonnet is perfect to match with the brown pelisse," Madame Furneaux declared, as she surveyed the young marchioness.

Valentina's expression, as she gazed into the mirror, was doubtful. "The colour is perhaps tolerable, but the feathers seem rather sparse, madame."

The Frenchwoman laughed. "That is nothing, my lady. The milliner will see that it is altered to please you."

"The gowns *will* be ready for Tuesday?" Valentina asked anxiously.

"*Mais oui.*" The woman flung her hands

up in the air. "You have my word on it, even though everyone, but *everyone*, wants gowns this week. Your waist, ma'am, is two entire inches larger than when I made your trousseau."

Valentina gave an impish look to her reflection in the mirror before saying, "My husband has been force-feeding me since our wedding."

The dressmaker laughed. A knock at the door heralded two men-servants. "You called, my lady?" enquired the senior of the two.

"Yes." She waved towards a statue in the corner of the room. "Please remove that, and when you have finished, move that table into the corner and the spinet nearer the centre of the room."

She turned to address the dressmaker then, "Don't forget I want more lace on the blue tansy."

"Yes, my lady, I forget nothing, but I cannot obtain French lace as you requested. You must be content with Flanders lace. No lace is coming from France. *C'est terrible.*"

Valentina nodded. "Very well. Flanders lace it will have to be, but remember as soon as you receive shipment of French lace I want to know."

"Yes, of course, madame. You are my most important client."

The servants returned to move the furniture and another followed close on their heels to announce, "Lady Woodville and Miss Daphne Woodville, my lady."

Valentina swept the new hat off her head. "Show them up quickly."

As the lackey went to do her bidding she gave the hat back to Madame Furneaux. "By Tuesday," she reiterated as she tidied her hair.

The woman bobbed a curtsey and was on her way out as Lady Woodville and Daphne came hurrying in.

"Mama! Daphne!" Valentina cried and rushed across the room to greet them.

Lady Woodville embraced her elder daughter before holding her away. "'Tis so good to see you back in Town, my dear, and looking so fine."

"And I am heartily glad to be back." Releasing herself she turned then to hug Daphne. "You look so grown-up. So wonderful."

Her sister's eyes twinkled. "I am making my debut this Season. Have you forgotten? My come out ball is on Friday."

"How could I forget?"

"We came as soon as we had word you had returned," Lady Woodville informed her.

"Life is so hectic," Valentina said breathlessly as her sister eyed her anxiously. "There is so much to arrange here at Stockdale House, gowns to purchase for the new Season, servants to organise. I have scarce had time to breathe."

Lady Woodville began to walk around the room watching the servants rearranging the furniture to Valentina's taste. "We, too, have been busy preparing for Daphne's come out. La! How I have come to enjoy it. I'd as lief have seven daughters as two."

"Papa would not," Valentina answered wryly.

"Oh, Papa. He declares his pockets are to let and he is about to be dunned by all the merchants in Town. It has always been so, let me tell you. Every time I purchased so much as a bolt of silk. If only Daphne's Season ends as well as yours I shall be more than happy and so will he.

"This is such a fine house." She turned

to gaze at her daughter again. "It relieves me to see you looking so well and you have put on weight. You look so robust. Can it be...?"

Valentina looked away, blushing slightly. "Mama!" she protested and then, taking Daphne's hand, "I'm so glad you will be out this Season, dearest. It could not be better for I intend to entertain lavishly; drums, routs, balls and breakfasts. You will be able to come, too!"

As Lady Woodville inspected the drawing room of her daughter's new home, a splendid house set back from the bustle and noise of Piccadilly, Daphne gazed anxiously at her sister.

"Valentina, I can scarce credit this change in you. Two months ago you were desolate at the prospect of marrying Lord Stockdale and now you are as gay as a goose in a gutter."

"Are you not pleased? Or would you as lief see me still wearing the willow?"

"I am delighted to see you in such high snuff and I beg you to tell me the reason for it. Has Lord Stockdale been transformed from frog to handsome prince?"

Her sister's laughter echoed around the

room. "Valentina!" her mother cried, peering into a cabinet, "This service is solid gold."

"I know, Mama." Then, turning to her sister, "Believe me when I tell you all is well. I can say no more."

Daphne looked petulant. "There were never any secrets between us before."

Valentina sighed. "I own I am bursting to tell someone."

"You can rely upon my discretion in all things."

Valentina glanced across the room at her mother who was examining a Greek statue. "Mama, I intend to ride in the Park this afternoon. Will you allow Daphne to accompany me?"

Lady Woodville came towards them. "What an excellent idea. Riding in the Park with the Marchioness of Stockdale can do your sister's aspirations nothing but good. Valentina, do you not think, whilst you are making alterations, that chair by the fire is a trifle ugly...?"

Her daughter's face dimpled mischievously. "No, Mama, it will have to remain."

Her mother looked miffed. "Very well, if you insist, although you have not enough

years for true taste. Come now, Daphne
dear, we must purchase a selection of gloves
whilst there is still a good choice to be had,
and I have no doubt your sister has a thou-
sand things to do."

Valentina blew Daphne a kiss. "I shall
call round this afternoon and we shall ride
at length in the Park."

As they reached the door it opened and
the marquis came in.

Taken aback, he did however recover
quickly. "Lady Woodville. Miss Woodville.
What a delightful surprise!"

He raised a hand of each to his lips in
turn. "Lord Stockdale," Lady Woodville
gushed, "I observe my daughter is looking
very well, but I am bound to say I believe
marriage suits you, too."

He inclined his head but not before he
had cast his wife what she thought to be a
malicious look. "I believe you are correct."

He then glanced around the room at the
rearranged furniture. "I see you have lost
no time in altering this room to suit yourself."

"You did say I might," she answered
defensively.

"Only because I was certain you would

deem it necessary and this is definitely a vast improvement. Do you not agree, Lady Woodville?"

"Indeed I do. Even though this room was always delightful it is also true that Valentina has such good taste, but perchance you can persuade her as I cannot that the tapestry chair in the corner is quite ugly and out of place amongst such exquisite pieces."

"Ah, the tapestry chair. That is my mother's own personal chair; she worked the cover herself as a young woman."

Lady Woodville's face was a picture of dismay as she began to splutter and stammer. Valentina turned away to hide a smile and she was certain Daphne giggled.

"However," the marquis went on a moment later, "I am inclined to agree with you and as my mother will not be here this Season, I think—do you not agree, my dear?—it should be removed."

"I have no objection," Valentina managed to answer and, mollified, Lady Woodville took her leave of them.

Left alone with her husband, Valentina's good spirits quickly evaporated. In all the two months of their marriage, alone except for servants in Hertfordshire, she had never become accustomed to his company which invariably discomforted her. That was why coming to London was such a joy; the social round was so hectic they need see so little of one another.

"I trust you have found everything in order," he asked, employing the expressionless tone which was customary when there was no one present to impress with their apparent devotion.

"Yes, indeed," she answered, turning to look out of the window.

As she did so he threw down a large handful of cards. "No one wishes to waste any time in issuing invitations to us. When you have decided which of them to accept send a list to my man of business and I shall ensure that I am free. I am sure you will know which of them warrant our attention. For the rest of the time you are free to do as you please."

"And you?" she asked, giving him a quick glance.

"I shall also be free to do as I please—naturally."

Valentina laced her fingers together

nervously. "Do you wish us to entertain here?"

"Naturally. Needless to say, as far as our social life is concerned you shall have a free hand in arranging entertainments. Merely have all the vouchers sent to me."

"You are very generous."

She heard him walk towards the door. "Not at all. 'Tis a matter of self interest, nothing more."

At this she turned, wishing to say something to him, but not knowing what.

Then, as he was about to take his leave of her, she burst out, "I am most grateful to you, Stockdale, for the freedom you intend to give me."

"It is my pleasure, ma'am," he answered with an urbane bow.

As the door closed behind him she waited only until the servants came to remove the dowager's chair before rushing to her room to change into an outfit suitable for a ride in the Park.

Six

"What a splendid piece of equipage!" Daphne exclaimed as she came out of her parents' house.

Her eyes opened wide at the sight of the brand new barouche, painted in green and gold with the Stockdale escutcheon on the door. A footman, clad in green and gold livery, hastened to open the door for her.

Valentina smiled at her sister's delight. "If we do not ride in style, I see no point in riding at all, Daphne."

As soon as the young lady sat down next to her sister, the carriage set off. Daphne's eyes sparkled.

"This morning I wondered if my eyes were deceiving me. You looked so fine and so happy."

"As you can see it is no dream," Valentina laughed. "Naturally I am all the better for being back in Town and so close to all those who mean everything to me."

Her sister looked abashed. "I have been a chuckle-head to fret over you, Valentina. Quite obviously you are well and happy. I can see that Stockdale is a doting husband, and I couldn't be more delighted that you have been proved wrong."

"Now, tell me about Stockdale House."

"It was horrendously boring," Valentina responded, affecting a fashionable languor.

"You always did dislike a rustic life, but is it very splendid?"

Her sister could not deny it. "The house is most congenial, Daphne. In all the time I was there I did not contrive to count all the rooms. The park is extensive, too. On clement days I walked for hours."

Her mind dwelled momentarily on the weeks she had spent at her husband's country estate, happiness about the future casting out any loneliness she might otherwise have felt. It had been, on reflection, a pleasant interlude coming after the physical demands of her first London Season, and the mental anguish which preceded her wedding.

True to his word, the marquis had not troubled her on any score. Most days he spent going about his business, shooting or fishing in his leisure time, and only at dinner did he and Valentina meet, parting afterwards to go about their separate pursuits. He never questioned Valentina about what she did in his absence and she was similarly silent about his pursuits. Now they had returned to London they need see each other even less which suited Valentina very well. Although she no longer hated the marquis, she still felt more relaxed and happy out of his presence.

"I cannot wait for a visit," Daphne enthused. "House parties there can only be brilliant."

For the first time Valentina's excitement faded a little, for she could hardly encourage her sister to believe there would be such entertainments, at least none presided over by her. By the end of the Season Stockdale would have put into effect the arrangements for an official separation.

The barouche entered the Park and from that moment onwards they had little time to converse, for the carriage was obliged to stop frequently by those anxious to greet the new marchioness. She had always been in great demand and Valentina discovered that she did not take amiss the new deference which was being given to her as the Marchionness of Stockdale.

Daphne squealed delightedly when she caught sight of their brother, Harry, riding towards them and at his side was none other than Viscount Mayne.

Valentina's heart began to beat loudly at her first sight of the man she loved since before her wedding. She would have preferred to have encountered him in a less public place but the pleasure of seeing him at all was just as great for all that.

"Val!" Harry cried as he approached. "Heard you were back. In fact, I've heard nothing else if you must know."

"You look very fine, Harry. That horse is no daisy cutter."

"She's a fine piece of blood, let me tell you, and cost me no small damage."

"You've changed your tailor, too. You've become quite the bang up blade."

"You can thank Stockdale for that. I can't take credit where it isn't due. Gave me an introduction to his tailor who's a splendid fellow."

Valentina was both surprised and pleased, but she was also very well aware that Lord Mayne was gazing at her all the time she was exchanging banter with her brother, and the knowledge caused colour to creep into her cheeks.

She turned to him at last, secure in the knowledge that her looks had never been better and her hat and pelisse of peach-coloured China silk flattered her colouring.

"Lord Mayne," she acknowledged, inclining her head.

"My lady, what a most fortunate encounter."

She affected indifference, a difficult feat, for inwardly joy and excitement bubbled up and threatened to betray her.

"Do you think so, my lord?"

"When I caught sight of you I could scarce believe such a vision of loveliness was real. The Town is aglow with your radiance, ma'am."

Her cheeks flushed, which only had the effect of heightening her beauty.

"You are an idle flatterer, Lord Mayne," she responded, laughing lightly.

Inwardly she rejoiced at his continuing devotion.

"Indeed I am not. I only wish my paltry words could do justice to you. There are not words enough in the English language to do that."

Valentina smiled, affecting boredom. She had no intention of encouraging him too much all at once. She must not seem too eager.

Turning to her sister she said, "You are acquainted with my sister, Lord Mayne."

Aware of his omission he hastened to make it good. "Of course. My pardon, Miss Woodville, but seeing Lady Stockdale so unexpectedly made me a trifle giddy. She and I are old friends."

Daphne smiled sweetly. "So I understand. Are you also an old friend of Lord Stockdale?"

The young man flushed and Harry said quickly, "Come along now, Mayne. We have a deal to do before dinner, so you'll be obliged to save your flummery for another day. Cheerio, ladies."

"Well, his tongue is certainly well-hung," Daphne declared as the two young men rode away. "'Tis no wonder you fancied yourself in love with him."

Silently Valentina watched them go and then gave the signal to drive on, hardly daring to speak lest she betray her inner joy. That, she realised, was going to be the real problem over the coming months— keeping the reason for her happiness a secret.

Aware that Daphne, who knew her far better than anyone else, was watching her curiously again Valentina turned to wave to an old acquaintance who was passing by.

"Valentina..." Daphne said in a quiet voice.

She turned to give her a wide and open smile. "Yes, dear?"

"There is something different about you."

Valentina waved to an old beau. "I am now the Marchioness of Stockdale. Would you have me act the hoyden?"

"It is something which goes far deeper than that," the girl insisted.

"You're mistaken. I am still the same person with whom you grew up."

"You were very mysterious this morning when Mama and I called in on you."

Valentina bit her lip with apprehension; although she longed to confide in her sister she was, nevertheless, afraid to do so.

"Valentina, when you married Lord Stockdale only two months ago," Daphne continued, "you behaved as though you were a French aristocrat going to her own execution. Now you return in such high snuff I cannot credit the change in you."

Valentina turned to her. "Oh, Daphne, I cannot hide my happiness from you of all people. You have always known the innermost secrets of my heart."

Her sister's worried frown cleared. "I am persuaded I do know what it is before you even speak."

"You do?" Valentina looked at her with wide-eyed astonishment.

The girl blushed and averted her eyes. Toying with her muff she said in almost a whisper, "Although you denied it this morning, I'm persuaded you are increasing, only you did not want Mama to know of it as yet." She looked up then, smiling happily.

"I am so pleased for you, Valentina. A child is exactly what you need."

"No!" Valentina cried, drawing back in horror. "I am not, and never likely to be."

Her sister became startled and began to stammer. "Oh, I am sorry, dearest. I was so certain... What else...? Why...? I cannot conceive what has put you in such high spirits."

After staring into her sister's troubled face for a moment or two Valentina said, "I must insist upon total secrecy, Daphne. Not a word of what I am about to tell you must ever pass your lips."

"Not all the torments of hell would draw it out of me."

Valentina's face relaxed and quickly she told her the essence of what she and the marquis had agreed, which caused Daphne to appear even more dismayed.

"You are most surely gammoning me," she gasped at last. "This must be a jest."

"Don't be such a chuckle-head. Why do you think I am so happy? I am no more enamoured of Stockdale than on my wedding day, and he is man enough to acknowledge we cannot deal well together in such circumstances."

The girl sank back into the squabs. "My ears must be deceiving me. Valentina, you cannot mean to go through with this abominable idea."

At this pronouncement Valentina laughed. "I certainly do. It is the answer to my prayers."

Daphne closed her eyes as if to shut out the terrible knowledge. "It will kill Mama."

"Fudge! She wished me a marchioness and so I am. Nothing will happen until you are safely leg-shackled yourself so she will have no cause to grumble."

She inclined her head to a passing acquaintance and Daphne was obliged to force a smile to her face. Then they stopped to exchange pleasantries with a couple in a curricle. As soon as they were able to move on once again Daphne's smile faded.

"What a buffle-head I must be to have thought you might have thrown your cap over the windmill for Lord Stockdale."

Valentina chuckled. "What a foolish notion indeed. As if I would. He is the last man on earth with whom I would fall in love."

"Nevertheless, you are married to him

and such a state involves certain obligations which you have obviously not fulfilled."

Valentina's cheeks grew pink again. "I hardly think we need to discuss it, Daphne. Stockdale is quite satisfied for our marriage to appear as it should."

"Valentina, I beg of you reconsider what you are about to do. The scandal will be mortifying."

"It will only be remembered until the next one comes along, and in any event I do not care a fig what the tattlebaskets may say."

Daphne drew a sigh of resignation. "As always, my love, I am persuaded you will have your way, but I cannot help thinking you will be obliged to fry in your own grease."

At such a dampening thought Valentina turned away from her sister in annoyance, only to catch sight, a distance away, of a high perch phaeton painted in similar colours to her own barouche, and tooling the ribbons with rare mastery was none other than her husband.

"Daphne, is that not Stockdale over there?"

From her rather shrivelled position,

Daphne once again sat up straight. "I do believe it is. What a splendid phaeton! Harry will be quite green with envy when he sees it and dash off to have one made for himself."

The phaeton was moving away from them and it appeared that the marquis had not seen his wife.

Valentina gripped her sister's arm with rather more ferocity than she would normally use. "Who is that creature at his side? I do declare I have seen her before."

Daphne obligingly peered into the distance and then her face cleared. "Indeed you have. That is Mirabelle Goodhayes, the widow of Sir Phineas Goodhayes, an old friend, I believe, of Lord Stockdale."

Valentina sank thoughtfully back into the squabs. "Ah, so it is. She is not the type of woman who remains in one's mind."

"Poor thing. No doubt Stockdale, out of the goodness of his heart, thought to bring her in his own conveyance. One must pity her."

Valentina gave the driver the order to leave the Park. "Why must I do that, Daphne?"

"Why, Sir Phineas left her widowed and

virtually penniless before she was even twenty, and then she had his child two months after the funeral."

"'Tis sad indeed," her sister agreed thoughtfully, and as the carriage drove out on to Park Lane she glanced back to catch a glimpse of her husband's phaeton disappearing into the distance.

Seven

Once again the house of Sir Arthur Woodville in Mount Street was a blaze of lights.
On this occasion the ball was held to cele-
brate the social debut of the younger Woodville girl.

The streets all around were choked
with carriages and in small groups, drivers
and link boys gathered together in the darkness to while away the long hours until
their masters and mistresses sent for them.

The sound of music and laughter could
be plainly heard, drifting along on the cool
night air in the street outside. Now and
again a passer-by would pause to listen and

93

perhaps to envy those with a coveted invitation to such a great social event.

Inside the house crowds milled through the various rooms, availing themselves of the abundant food and drink, the variety of card games or, as favoured by the younger guests, dancing to the orchestra which played on inexorably.

Although Daphne Woodville was not held to be as handsome as her sister, it was generally acknowledged that with her pleasing demeanour and generous portion, she could not fail to make a good match.

Watching her two daughters, the younger dancing with a new admirer and the elder in conversation with a group of people which included her husband, Lady Woodville's ample bosom swelled with pride and satisfaction, and she could not help but remark upon it to her husband.

"It was such a splendid sight seeing both our girls presented to Her Majesty, Daphne as a debutante and dear Valentina as the Marchioness of Stockdale."

"Yes, I am obliged to admit you have done well in raising our brood, Grizelda. A relief, too, to see Valentina reconciled to her marriage. I admit I did not expect it to be so. Our elder daughter can be deucedly self-willed when she chooses." He chuckled. "I do not, in all conscience, envy Stockdale, but I do admire the fellow. He has our hoyden behaving very prettily."

He ambled off happily to refill his glass and at the same time Valentina caught sight of Lady Goodhayes standing alone, and purposefully moved around the room in order to approach her. Since seeing the widow with her husband, the vision had stayed with her and it was not an easy memory. Valentina had never entertained any illusions about Stockdale's morals, and she would not have been surprised to see him in the company of some accredited beauty or a fashionable impure. However, this woman whose figure tended to be shapeless and whose face was rather less than beautiful, was not at all what she would expect to see in his company.

"Lady Goodhayes, are you enjoying the ball?"

The widow smiled sweetly on being addressed by Valentina. "Indeed, I am, Lady Stockdale. All is quite splendid and Sir Arthur and Lady Woodville are to be congratulated. They must feel a great deal of satisfaction tonight."

"I am certain that they do. I believe you are an acquaintance of my husband."

"My own late husband was a close friend of Lord Stockdale. I am bound to say, however, that after his passing, Lord Stockdale became an invaluable ally to me, and I only wish I knew a way to repay his kindness."

Valentina smiled as she swished her fan to and fro. "Oh, I am persuaded your devotion is all the payment he craves."

"If that is so I am the most fortunate of creatures," she declared, unaware of the irony in Valentina's voice.

"Do I intrude on the latest *on dit*?"

She turned on her heel to come face to face with the marquis himself who had come upon them unheard. Valentina bit back a gasp of annoyance but Lady Goodhayes laughed.

"Nothing so mundane, my lord."

Valentina was not at all pleased at the interruption, for she had hoped to question the woman further and in privacy in the hope of learning more about her relationship with the marquis, something which was beginning to intrigue her.

However, she merely looked at him askance. "Lady Goodhayes was assailing me with news of your good deeds on her behalf."

"What a most tedious topic on which to converse. Can you not find something more interesting?"

"No!" the widow assured him with a smile. "You may be the epitome of all that is modest, but I declare Lady Stockdale has a right to know of it."

"Oh, my dear," he answered, smiling wryly, "I am quite persuaded that is not what my wife wishes to hear."

"Any wife would want to hear that her husband is all goodness and condescension."

Valentina noted that this woman was totally at ease with the marquis, something which did not, somehow, please her. In fact, their easy rapport distinctly irritated her.

"*Many* wives, Lady Goodhayes, not any," he countered and she laughed again.

"Fudge! Is that not so, Lady Stockdale?"

"Any wife would indeed be delighted to learn something which she does not already know."

"Oh, I am persuaded you are already aware that Lord Stockdale is everything that is good." She turned to the gentleman in question, her eyes sparkling. "I reiterate that any wife would rejoice in such news."

Valentina was growing heartily tired of this light banter, feeling that there was a good deal she did not know of their relationship, save that it was an easy one.

The marquis looked at the woman with what Valentina recognised as mock-seriousness. "I can assure you, my dear, there are those who would not hear a word of good on their spouse's behalf."

"And I am bound to say Lady Stockdale cannot possibly be one of them."

"It would seem," Valentina cut in as she could bear no more of it, "my husband has set himself up as an expert on the working of the female mind."

His eyes sparkled with malicious amusement. "No man alive can fathom the workings of the female mind let alone study it."

Lady Goodhayes laughed again. "Shame on you, Stockdale! That is a shabby thing to say."

Vexedly Valentina began to swish her

fan once more before making a brief curtsey. "You must excuse me from further comment upon the subject; I am engaged for the minuet."

She strode away from them, still angry at her exclusion from their easy rapport. When she paused to glance back at them they were still in animated conversation, his face relaxed as never in her company. In fact, it was a revelation to her, for at such times he looked almost dashing.

"Lady Stockdale..."

When she looked up, her thoughts were immediately diverted from her husband's relationship with his friend's widow, for Lord Mayne was gazing down at her.

Immediately she opened her fan to hide her confusion and held it up to her face.

"Lady Stockdale, are you not engaged for the next set?"

"I believe so," she answered coolly, "although I would as lief cry off."

He was visibly taken aback and she went on, "The night is exceeding warm, Lord Mayne, and I would as lief take a turn on the balcony as join the set."

At this pronouncement he appeared a little relieved. "As you wish."

He escorted her down the stairs and through one of the card rooms.

"I have gained the distinct impression you are displeased with me, Lady Stockdale," he said as they reached the cool and quiet of the garden balcony.

"I am gratified that you have noted it," she answered, still retaining her cool tone towards him.

"My lady, I am at a loss to know how I may have displeased you."

"I have been in Town for all of a sen'night and although half the *haut monde* has called in at Piccadilly I have yet to receive such a call from you."

He turned away, gazing out into the lantern-festooned gardens where several guests dallied. "You should not be surprised, or angry although I am aware I am deserving of a set-down from you on this score."

She began to swish her fan to and fro, not because she needed the air, but to hide her own uncertainty and fear.

"You have no doubt a deal of business which needs your attention. I am a chucklehead to expect you to spare a few moments for me."

He turned to her then, his eyes ablaze
with passion. "You don't know what you
say! If I have been remiss in not calling upon
you 'tis only because I cannot bear the pain
of knowing you are lost to me for ever."

Valentina's heart began to beat fast
again. "Oh, my dear, you relieve me. I
feared that you have become indifferent to
me, which I own is selfish but my heart is
constant, believe me."

He clasped her hands in his. "This is
indeed a wonderful and yet heart-breaking
moment. My dear Valentina—how I have
longed to speak your name aloud!—I have
never minced words with you and I shall
not begin to do so now." She looked up at
him questioningly, her eyes alight with ad-
oration. "It is imperative that I seek a wife.
My heart will always belong to you, beloved,
but I want you to know this and understand.
If I pay court to another it will not alter my
feelings for you."

The pain evident upon his face was not
matched by hers. "Only wait," she begged.
"Do not rush into some ill-advised match,
I beg of you."

At last he let go of her hands and turned
away again. "My aunt on whose favour I am

obliged to rely is insisting that I become·leg-shackled to some worthy female. The fact that I am in love with a married lady will not weigh with her, and understandably so."

Valentina put her hand on his arm as he kept his head averted. "There is hope yet for us."

"Even if we become lovers I shall still be obliged to take a wife who is not to my fancy."

"You are quite wrong." She toyed with her fan for a moment before saying in a soft voice, "I know I ought not to tell you this, but I can rely upon your discretion..."

"Always," he vowed, gazing at her curiously.

She took a deep breath then before saying, "At the end of this Season, Stockdale and I are to separate." He stared at her in amazement and she was forced to laugh. "Yes, 'tis true. He recognises that our marriage was a mistake and is willing to give me my freedom."

"I cannot credit this."

She laughed again, her heart feeling light. "But is it not the most wonderful news?"

He still looked bewildered. "I never imagined that this could happen."

"Nor I but 'tis true. Stockdale is a man of honour and I trust his word. We shall part at the end of the Season for ever and I will be free to come to you. Say you are pleased, dearest."

"There is something not quite right about this, Valentina. I feel it in my bones."

She drew back from him, indignant that he should not share her delight. "You are not pleased. Oh, I have been most roundly fooled by all your pretty speeches, Lord Mayne."

He caught her hand as she would have left him. "No! No, do not say such a thing. If there was a chance for us I would declare myself the happiest man in the world."

"Have I not been telling you that the future can be ours if only you will wait a few months?"

Still he refused to display his pleasure at the prospect. "He has used you, my love. Do you really believe Lord Stockdale would be so benevolent? I cannot credit that you have been so simple-minded in all this."

Again she drew back. "Lord Mayne, you go too far!"

Bewildered and hurt by his attitude, she would have turned and walked away from him, only he caught her arm and retained her.

"Before you and he were wed he paid court to the widow of Phineas Goodhayes."

"This is nothing I do not already know," she answered icily, nonetheless angered to realise it was general knowledge.

"Lady Goodhayes is practically penniless."

"So I am aware."

"Do you not see that if you and he are divorced, he will still retain the right to your portion and will then be free to wed this woman?"

She smiled faintly. "My husband is hardly in need of my portion, Lord Mayne. He is a wealthy man in his own right."

"How do you know?"

"I beg your pardon?"

"Stockdale gambles deep and I have seen him lose heavily myself. How do you know the state of his finances? It may have been imperative for him to marry an heiress, not just a desirability. After all, he has not hurried into wedlock before now."

"This is pure speculation, Lord Mayne, and I may say I find it distasteful."

"Nevertheless, you must face it. Lady Goodhayes gave birth to a son two months after her husband expired."

"There is nothing untoward in that, as you well know."

"Sir Phineas was bedbound for a twelvemonth before he died."

Valentina was momentarily startled but then she approached him again. "What does any of this matter? If my husband loves another it is nothing to me. Indeed it is most fortunate. We can be happy together and that is all which matters."

He averted his eyes and she began to feel panic welling up inside her. "Tell me that you will wait until I am free, Oliver." Still he did not answer or look at her. "Tell me!"

"You have been accustomed to everything of the best, my dear," he said at last in a sad voice. "You would not survive long in the penury marriage to me would provide." He raised her hand to his lips as she gazed at him, her eyes filled with pain and disbelief. "You must excuse me now, my dear. The music strikes up and I am engaged for this set with your sister."

"Daphne," she whispered, as he let her hand drop.

"May I escort you back inside the house first?"

She turned her head away. "No! Go! Leave me alone."

He bowed curtly. "As you wish, but I beg of you to believe I shall always be devoted to you and wish you happy. It would be advantageous to both of us if you remained married to Stockdale. He will allow you enough freedom to pursue your own fancy."

He left her in no doubt about what he meant. She stayed motionless until his footsteps signalled his departure and then she allowed the tears to slide down her cheeks. Despair tore at her heart. Both men had betrayed her. From basking in the love of many men she discovered she possessed the heart of none. And without doubt, Valentina acknowledged, it was her own doing, but that did not lessen her heartbreak.

Sobs racked her body as she gave rein to a despair which hadn't seized her even when she knew marriage to the marquis was unavoidable.

A step on the balcony caused her to choke back further tears but when she realised it was the marquis she drew back into the shadows in a desperate attempt to avoid being seen by him. Too late though; after a moment he caught sight of her.

"Valentina, is that you?"

She did not answer for fear she would sob out the words. Once again hatred of this man rose up in her throat almost to choke her. Until that moment she had had no notion how treacherous men could be. Neither of them had wanted her for herself alone, and the knowledge was shattering.

"Why are you out here?"

"I needed to take the air," she murmured as he came towards her.

"You might well contract a severe chill if you dally here for much longer."

"Then that will be too bad."

"You must not be so heedless of your health, Valentina."

He was standing close to her now, so close she hardly dared to breathe.

"Are you certain you are not already ill? You seem sadly out of sorts."

"I am perfectly well," she retorted in a muffled voice, resenting his solicitude as much as she would his indifference.

After a moment he reached out and, cupping his hand beneath her chin, turned her face round to gaze into his.

He inspected her features carefully before saying, "Why, your cheeks are wet with tears, my dear. Has something happened to put you out of contenance?"

She jerked her head back, hating the concern in his voice which she was convinced could not be genuine.

"'Tis nothing. A mere speck in my eye which proves stubborn to remove."

"In that case you must allow me to assist you."

She tried to back away but the balustrade defeated her objective. "Pray do not trouble; 'tis nothing."

"Anything which causes you such distress cannot be deemed as nothing."

He drew out a fine lawn handkerchief and with his free hand turned her face towards the light. "Now, madam, where is the trouble?"

"Here," she relented, "in the left eye."

His face was close to hers and once

again her breath came only with difficulty as her heart beat a loud tattoo. After a moment, which seemed like an eternity, he drew away, saying with satisfaction, "I believe I have it." He smiled. "Only a tiny speck."

Valentina sighed with relief as he drew away, triumphantly holding up the handkerchief. "Now you can return inside. Several anxious gentlemen are waiting to partner you. Perchance you have one set free later."

She walked with him across the balcony not quite yet composed. Oddly enough it was her encounter with the marquis rather than the one with Lord Mayne which served to disconcert her more.

At one time she would have claimed a full programme, but suddenly she was moved to show everyone who knew about Lady Goodhayes that her husband was not entirely indifferent to her, and that Lord Mayne's craven behaviour did not matter a jot.

"The gavotte," she suggested, "unless, of course, you are engaged for that one."

"I am engaged for several sets," he admitted, "but I doubt if it will be difficult to extricate myself from one of them. After all," he added, casting her a smile, "We must endeavour to present to the world a picture of married bliss."

Eight

"How does that please you, my lady?"

Valentina gazed into the dressing table mirror as the hairdresser dusted powder on to her curls.

"The colour becomes me better than the last one you applied, Mr. Dunnett; I own that it is very pleasing. However," she added with a smile, "you have imparted little scandal during this visit and that is most unlike you."

"Alas since Lord Crampton's daughter eloped with his lordship's house steward, and Lord Gible gamed away his inheritance there is little to be told, ma'am; at least from those who patronise *me*. All seems to be concerned with the inordinate numbers of Frenchies swarming over the Town."

Her smile faded at the reminder of the terrible happenings across the Channel.

"One can scarce believe such tales of barbarism," she murmured.

"They are true, my lady, you can rely upon that. I hear them first hand from those who have suffered."

She reached for her patch box and selected two. As she began to apply them to her cheeks she said, "One cannot help but wonder if such an uprising could possibly happen here."

The hairdresser drew back in horror. "I hope not, my lady, if only for the sake of my own neck, for in France those who serve the Quality are dealt with as severely as their masters."

At this she smiled. "What a craven creature you are to be sure, Mr. Dunnit."

He removed her powdering robe and as she got to her feet, he said, "I go now to Mount Street to dress Miss Woodville's hair. She favours a lighter powder than you do, my lady."

"Her complexion is paler than mine, Mr. Dunnit."

"Oh, I always say that only Lady Stockdale comes near to perfection. Her hair is a joy to dress."

Valentina looked at him wryly. "Mr. Dunnit, you are a tongue pad. You fill all your clients with flummery."

"If I do, Lady Stockdale, it does not mean I am not truthful about you."

She moved away from the dressing table as he began to gather up his combs and pins.

"Mr. Dunnit," she said artlessly, "does my sister talk to you a great deal whilst you dress her hair?"

"Miss Woodville is a chatter-box, Lady Stockdale, as you may know."

"Oh, indeed, but she has a young lady's love of secrecy where matters of the heart are concerned and I am longing to discover which of her suitors she favours most."

She spoke lightly but in the weeks since her sister's come out ball Valentina had become uneasily aware that Lord Mayne did intend to pursue the younger Woodville girl with as much gusto as he had payed court to Valentina herself. What is more there was every sign that Daphne was encouraging him.

Losing him was quite bad enough but if it was to be her own sister it would become unbearable. This, selfishly, was her prime concern although there was also a deepseated desire within her to prevent Daphne being tied to so shallow a man.

"Let me see," the man mused as he waved an ivory comb in the air. "Mr. Osgood called one day when I was there and Miss Woodville was exceeding pleased to see him."

"Are there no titles in evidence?" she ventured.

"There is one of whom she speaks more often than most, I recall. Viscount Mayne is a favourite."

At this confirmation Valentina was obliged to force a smile to her lips. "It is only what I suspected—and feared."

"He has paid court to many of my ladies to no avail, but one who has such address is bound to be successful eventually." He bowed as he prepared to leave. "Until the morrow, my lady."

Valentina had little opportunity to brood

about this snippet of information before a footman sought her out.

"Lord Ireton craves your indulgence, my lady."

"Oh, do show him up," she responded, glad of any diversion.

The fop came bustling into her boudoir. "My dear Lady Stockdale, how fortunate I am to find you at home."

"Fortunate indeed, for 'tis only because my hairdresser has just finished."

"I passed him on the stairs. I doubt, however, if even he can improve on perfection."

Valentina dimpled as she indicated he should be seated. His mode of dress, brocade coat with paste buttons and a wig dressed high at the front, left much to be desired, but he never failed to amuse her and of late Valentina found she needed such people around her.

"I do hope you have come to divert me with some amusing *on dit*, Lord Ireton."

He looked taken aback. "I have come only to feast my eyes upon your loveliness, my dear."

She laughed lightly. "That might well be enough for *you*, my lord, but think of *me*."

"Well, here is a small *on dit* for you,"
he said, lowering his voice. "Helena Crimpleton has taken Belton as her gallant at
last. He has been in pursuit, as you well
know, for weeks."

Valentina was taken aback, for the girl
was wed as recently as herself.

"It is well known, of course, that she
and Crimpleton dislike each other heartily,
and Crimpleton still keeps his Cyprian in
Bloomsbury. He sees more of her than his
wife, so one really cannot blame the chit."
He looked at Valentina speculatively and
she could no longer affect gaiety. Then he
said, "Your devotion to your husband makes
it exceeding frustrating for those of us who
would be *your* gallant, my lady."

She managed to force a laugh. "Oh,
Lord Ireton, how flattering. You are too
kind."

"No one could be too kind to you,
ma'am," and then after a pause he ventured,
"I note that Mayne is still in pursuit of Miss
Woodville." She started at the mere mention of his name. "They were seen driving
together yesterday in the Park."

This news concerned her more than any
other for such an outing only proved that

Daphne's feelings for the viscount were serious. When the clock on the mantel struck the hour she took the opportunity of jumping to her feet.

"You must forgive me, my lord, but I have an appointment with my dressmaker, and you know how temperamental these French women can be."

With obvious reluctance the man took his leave of her and as soon as he did so her false smile faded and she called for Mary to fetch her outdoor clothes.

She had just pinned on her hat when a lackey gave her the news:

"Lord Stockdale craves your presence in the library, my lady."

As Valentina rarely saw her husband save for the necessity of appearing together at public functions this summons came as something of a surprise, and not a very welcome one either.

She was still stung by Lord Mayne's revelations about the marquis and Lady Goodhayes, of which she had been unaware until then, and as it seemed all too likely the knowledge hurt her deeply.

"Tell Lord Stockdale I am about to go

out, and have my carriage brought round immediately."

When she came downstairs a short time later, wearing her hat, pelisse and outdoor shoes, the marquis came to the door of the library in which he conducted most of his business.

"Madame, your presence, if you please."

He thrust open the library door and Valentina was about to resist further when she realised his demeanour had a steely look about it which brooked any further resistance by her.

Reluctantly and less than pleased at such an arbitrary summons she walked past him into the library, her head held high.

The desk was littered with documents. The marquis's man of business was also present, but after bowing to Valentina he gathered up some of the documents and bowed out of the room.

"Please be seated, my dear."

She sat down, not at all fooled by his pleasant tone. She had the distinct feeling he was angry about something and that she was to be the recipient of his displeasure.

"I trust you will not detain me for long, Stockdale."

"No longer than is necessary, my dear," he answered, regarding her for a long moment.

His coat, she noted, was of the finest stuff and immaculately cut, his neck cloth pristine white. His stature seemed to have grown since she had first come to know him, although she realised that was a nonsense, for he had not changed at all. It seemed more likely that it was she who had.

"I have several calls to make," she told him as he strode across the room towards her."

"Of the utmost import, naturally."

"As a matter of fact, they are," she answered, aware of his sarcasm.

She watched as he took a pinch of snuff from the mother of pearl box on his desk. "No doubt the Strand mercers will await your custom a little longer."

"I was about to visit my mother."

He immediately looked concerned. "She is not ill, I trust?"

"As far as I am aware she is perfectly robust."

He gave her a half smile. "Good. Then I am not detaining you from a desperate mission. Your bonnet, incidentally, is very fetching."

Swallowing her irritation, she asked, "My lord, do you or do you not have something to impart to me?"

He drew himself up straighter and looked down his highbridged nose at her. "I trust you are settling down here and have no complaints of any nature."

"If I had you would have heard about them by now. After all, we have been in residence here some three months now."

"I am glad to hear you are so well settled, but that makes me even more puzzled about some *on dits* which have reached my ears."

Valentina looked at him expectantly and he went on, clasping his hands behind his back and fixing her with a steely look which was most disconcerting.

"It seems that the salons are buzzing with the rumour that you and I are about to separate..."

She started and he continued in an even voice which frightened her more than his anger would. "As no word of it has passed my lips since the day of our wedding, I cannot help but wonder why such a rumour should have started."

There was a momentary silence before she answered in an uneven voice with feigned lightness, "*On dits* are for ever circulating. Most of them are totally untrue but occasionally one inadvertently touches a vein of truth."

"I trust that you are right about that, my dear, for if I thought you had been indiscreet, I should be severely displeased."

"Have you no notion who started the rumour?" she asked hesitantly a moment later.

"All my attempts to trace it back to its source have met with failure."

Valentina could only experience a feeling of relief on that score, but her mind was in a whirl. It was calamitous that the salons of the *ton* should be buzzing with talk of their marriage. Daphne would not, under pain of death, reveal what she had been told so it had to be Lord Mayne who had spread the rumour and betrayed her trust in him. Inwardly she fumed, not so much for his betrayal of her trust, but because she, herself, had been such a fool. She had rarely been taken in by anyone as she had by that poltroon.

The marquis came round to the front of the desk and seated himself on its edge. He was altogether too close to her for comfort now and when he asked, "What are we to do to dispel such rumours?" she got to her feet and began to pace the room.

"I cannot imagine. I believe we have already done everything possible to present a happy face to our friends."

"Evidently we have not done enough."

At last she could contain herself no longer. "Mayhap your appearance at every turn with Lady Goodhayes leads people to form the opinion there is more than friendship between you."

His look of outrage might have mollified her had not his eyes retained the light of mockery in them.

"Do you really believe it is my innocent behaviour which has given rise to this nonsense?"

Valentina drew herself up proudly. "I can think of no other reason."

He got to his feet then, slapping his knee as he did so. "By jove, you are right, Valentina! Who would ever have conceived that an old and valued friendship with the widow of my greatest friend could be misconstrued so roundly?"

Her lips twisted into the travesty of a smile. "Everything is misconstrued in the circles in which we move."

"Then, obviously, we must be at pains to put the matter to rights. What do you suggest we do, Valentina?"

She shrugged her shoulders. "I cannot say. Mayhap we go about our separate lives too much after all. It might be as well to attend more functions in each other's company."

"If that is what you believe we must do, then so be it." She stared at him in astonishment and he went on, mockingly again. "Do you believe you can bear such a burden? Can you hide your dislike of me sufficiently well?"

"But of course," she stammered, hating his obvious ridicule, "if it is what you think right."

"I do. We have obviously not acted in the correct manner of late. That's settled."

Valentina didn't know whether to be alarmed or relieved. She was certainly not pleased at the prospect of having the marquis at her elbow more than necessary, for she had been enjoying male approbation more now than in her come out year, and many of the gentlemen showering her with compliments and gifts were very much to her taste. However, she did acknowledge that she had escaped his anger when it was her own indiscretion which must be to blame for the rumour.

Breathlessly she glanced at him, as she effected to straighten her hat, "Well, if that is settled..."

"Tales of our unfashionable devotion will soon replace those stories of a rift," he promised, and then he added, "before you go I have some more news to impart." She looked at him in alarm as he waved a piece of parchment in the air. "I have today received this communication from an old friend of mine."

"Not another widow of a great friend," she mocked.

"This is not amusing, Valentina. The Comte de Fontaine has just arrived in England."

Her ironic smile faded. "An emigré?"

"He was arrested but contrived to escape his guards and fled the country."

"Poor man," she murmured, genuinely moved.

"He has sent word to me and I have invited him to stay here for the time being."

London was being flooded with the pathetic refugees from the Revolutionary Terror, and although Valentina, like everyone else, felt for them deeply the *beau monde* was all too well aware that France was a mere twenty-five miles from England and what had happened there could so easily happen here.

"You've invited him to stay with us here at Piccadilly?" she asked incredulously.

"Did I not say that?"

"Why?"

"Because he is in need of a refuge," the marquis argued, his eyes snapping with anger.

It had rarely been directed towards her and Valentina found she did not like it at all.

"His presence will play havoc with our social life, and that is precisely what you do not want."

"I cannot acknowledge that."

"Why can he not lodge somewhere in St. James's?"

The marquis threw down the letter. "He has not a penny piece with which to bless himself. He has written to me from Dover because he has not the money to travel to London. I have already dispatched a carriage to bring him here. Have you no charity in you, Valentina?"

Her eyes were downcast. "I beg your pardon, Stockdale. It was thoughtless of me. I shall have a suite made ready for him."

"I am obliged. His situation may not be as bad as I fear, but we will know better his true position when he arrives."

She nodded and turned to go. Just as she did so, he said, "We have been wed now for half a year, Valentina."

For some reason a lump rose in her throat and she could not turn to face him. Instead she said, affecting a light tone, "La! Does not time fly past quickly?"

"But not quickly enough, eh?" he mocked.

Valentina still could not meet his mocking gaze, nor could she reply and before he could say anything more she sketched a curtsey and hurried from the room. Once she was out in the hall she was surprised to discover her cheeks damp.

"Your carriage awaits, my lady," a footman informed her.

"I don't require it any longer," she told him in a choked voice before running up the stairs to the sanctuary of her own room where she could examine the tumult of her own tortured emotions alone.

Nine

The rout held at Stockdale House was in full swing. Dancing, gaming and general conversation was being pursued with much gusto in several rooms of the house.

Valentina glanced about her and experienced a feeling of great satisfaction, knowing the function she had arranged was being acknowledged as one of the best of the Season.

Becoming a Society hostess came naturally to her and despite the strange state of her marriage, she had enjoyed this aspect of her duties. It was the one thing she would miss once her marriage was over.

However, that was something she tried not to think about too much of late, for the prospect no longer was such an inviting one. As the Marchioness of Stockdale, she was eagerly sought by the hostesses of the *ton* as were her own invitations. As a divorced woman most would shun her and although she had never considered this earlier, now the notion irked. She had come to enjoy her position of influence.

When she caught sight of her mother and sister, Valentina thrust such discomforting thoughts from her mind and rushed forward to greet them.

"Daphne, my dear, you look quite ravishing."

"I shall never rival you, my love."

"Consider yourself fortunate," Valentina couldn't help but respond.

Her sister smiled uncertainly. "Yes, as a matter of fact I do."

A beau came to claim her for a dance and Lady Woodville drew her elder daughter to the edge of the floor.

"My dear, I must confess I have been most gratified to see Stockdale so often at your side of late."

Valentina could not meet her mother's probing gaze. "Why is that, Mama?"

"I see no reason not to tell you I had heard some ridiculous *on dit* regarding the state of your marriage. Needless to say, being also aware of your attitude towards Stockdale before you were wed I was most concerned. I hope you can assure me that all is truly well between you."

Still Valentina could not look directly at her mother and was glad there was much to distract both of them. "Naturally, Mama, as you have observed. Unfortunately, during my betrothal I was less than discreet about my attitude towards Stockdale, and some envious creature is making mischief of that."

"That is quite consistent with some of those we know," Lady Woodville responded in a scathing tone of voice. "At least your father and I can be content in the knowledge Stockdale is a splendid fellow and you have come to your senses. Your marriage is a great success and no one can fail to see it."

Catching sight of Daphne at that moment with Lord Mayne, Valentina began to grow irritated. "Mama, mayhap you and Papa had best concern yourself with

Daphne's well-being rather than mine. It seems to me Lord Mayne is paying court to her in earnest, and Daphne is very receptive to his charms."

"The choosing of a suitable spouse is not for you or I to decide. Sir Arthur will do so, but in all honesty, Valentina, we cannot possibly hope for as brilliant a match as yours."

Such bland utterances only served to increase Valentina's vexation and that wasn't helped by the sight of the marquis wearing his new evening coat with gold buttons, entering the room with Lady Goodhayes on his arm. Nor was she the only person to note it; their entrance invited a good deal of interest from all sides.

Lady Woodville frowned, too, when she saw them and Valentina suspected her mother had also heard the *on dits* circulating about the pair. It was, she thought, at this point that the prospect of a separation began to lose its attraction. A divorce which would enable her to marry the man she really loved was one thing, but one which would allow the marquis to marry whom he really preferred was too galling to contemplate.

If the marquis did marry Lady Goodhayes in the fullness of time and so legiti-
mise their son, the result would be total
humiliation for Valentina who had no child.
At the very thought of it tears of anger and
frustration began to prick at her eyes and
as the couple approached she could have
stamped her foot with vexation.

"Lady Stockdale, allow me to congrat-
ulate you on such a superb hurricane," the
widow greeted her. "I have heard nought
but complimentary reports on the evening's
events."

"I thank you, Lady Goodhayes." She
glanced scathingly at her husband who
seemed to be, by comparison, in excellent
spirits. "It appears that you find everything
to your satisfaction."

"I was only just now telling Lord Stockdale that simply because you are a consci-
entious hostess does not mean you cannot
yourself join in the fun."

"Lady Goodhayes has called me remiss
in not standing up with you as yet," her
husband confided.

Lady Woodville looked as affronted as
her daughter. "Do you always obey Lady
Goodhayes's strictures, Lord Stockdale?"

The marquis smiled urbanely, not at all put out. "Not always, Lady Woodville, but on this occasion I believe I shall." He looked at Valentina then. "By your leave, my dear?"

Valentina closed her fan with a snap and allowed him to lead her on to the floor where sets were being made up for the next dance.

As he bowed and she curtseyed at the beginning of the set he said, "Lady Goodhayes is quite correct when she says you are an excellent hostess."

"Is not Lady Goodhayes always correct?" she responded, her voice heavy with irony.

"Why have I gained the distinct impression that you have taken Lady Goodhayes in dislike?"

Again the mockery which angered her, but she was determined not to give in to the irritation which she was certain he wished her to do.

"My lord," she answered in shocked tones, "if I have given such an impression it is an entirely false one."

"You relieve me," he answered, smiling again.

At this point she cast him a curious look. "Is it so important that I should like her?"

"Not important," he answered after a moment's thought, "but it would please me if you and she were to become friends. She would be a constant friend and correct me if I am mistaken in saying you will be in need of one in the future."

She almost laughed at the notion, although she could see how convenient such a situation might be.

"I noticed that Georgiana Devonshire and Lady Elizabeth Foster are both here and in good spirits," she couldn't help but say, alluding to the Duke's wife and mistress, all of whom lived beneath the same roof.

The marquis gazed across the room to where the three sat contentedly together and then he looked at his wife again.

"They are, most certainly, but I wonder why you have seen fit to mention it when no one any longer finds it remarkable."

"Lady Devonshire is a remarkably tolerant lady."

"No more than many others and she has her own interests."

Valentina was vexed again for she was not winning any trump cards in this game of wits. It was a new sensation for her.

The minuet ended, much to her relief, and after bowing to her formally at its close the marquis led her across the floor.

"I must ascertain that all is in readiness for supper to be served," she said, almost shyly.

"I am certain that it is. You have our servants trained to the finest degree possible."

Her cheeks flushed slightly at his praise, aware that he was gazing at her admiringly, something which caused her no pleasure in the past but which certainly pleased her now.

"What a pity Providence has not seen fit to smile upon our union," he murmured.

She looked up at him, fearful now, as he relinquished her hand. "Together we could have set the Town alight."

"Alex..." she began, not really knowing what to say, but in any event he had begun to move away.

"Lady Torrington may not dance as well as you, my dear, but she has promised the next set to me and I am obliged to seek her out."

Valentina watched him go, not knowing whether she was relieved or sorry, but she had little time to ponder on the puzzle before she was claimed for the next set. However, his enigmatic and teasing words haunted her for the remainder of the evening.

The very next day Valentina called in at Mount Street in the hope of discovering for herself the true state of her sister's affections, especially with regard to a certain viscount who was making himself indispensable to her.

With thoughts—and not very kind ones—of Lord Mayne in her mind it came as a shock to meet him coming out of her parents' house as she climbed down from her carriage. She was not very pleased at the encounter and as he nodded stiffly to her it seemed he was not in his usual high spirits either.

"Lady Stockdale," he greeted her. "Valentina," he added in a lower voice which did nothing to ease her resentment towards him.

She inclined her head curtly and scarce paused as she responded, "Good day to you, Lord Mayne."

"I have displeased you," he said then, as she made to go past him.

At this she paused and smiled. "Displeased me, Lord Mayne? I assure you that is not so."

A faint smile flickered across his face. "I am deeply relieved to hear you say so, ma'am."

"You need never have a fear of displeasing me," she continued in a pleasant voice, "for there is no way in which you can influence my feelings in any direction."

Once more she inclined her head in a dismissive gesture and strode into the house. As the door closed behind her the derisory smile faded.

Daphne, she discovered, was on her own in the drawing room, which surprised her. Her sister's eyes were aglow and her face radiant as she came to greet Valentina.

"Oh, how fine you look, dearest!"

"It is icy cold out there and really not fit for travelling. I was so certain my nose is red."

"Not at all."

"One of the horses almost slipped on

Bond Street and there could have been a nasty accident. The roads are so icy more sawdust will have to be put down if accidents are going to be avoided."

Daphne beamed at her. "Well, I am so glad you decided to brave the cold and call on me. It's been devilishly dull here today."

"Where is Mama?"

"She awoke with the headache this morning and Posy gave her some laudanum. She will stay in her room for the day, I fear."

Valentina was naturally sorry to hear of her mother's indisposition and yet it was providential that she be given this opportunity to talk with her sister in privacy.

"If she does not recover soon have no fear for your engagements, dear. I shall chaperone you whenever it is necessary."

Daphne sat down on the edge of a sofa, her silk skirts flowing over the edge. Her sister eyed her wryly, sensing the change which social success had wrought in the girl.

"How fortunate I am to have so important a personage as my sister. I am persuaded that my Season would not have been so successful if it were not for your importance, my love."

"Fudge! Your own delightful nature and pretty manners have ensured your success and nothing else."

Daphne's eyes sparkled mischievously. "Perchance my portion is a little to do with it, too. In any event," she went on with scarce a pause, "your rout was a great success. I declare no one has ever seen the like before."

Valentina sat down, too, stripping off her gloves slowly. "It was obvious the evening was a great success for *you*."

"Oh yes, indeed. The evening passed like a dream. I was not obliged to sit out one set."

Valentina looked at her again. "You stood up on more than one occasion with Lord Mayne, I noted."

Daphne's cheeks grew pink at the reminder. "He is very persistent, Valentina."

"Yes, I know," she answered with a sigh.

"Only moments before you arrived he called here, but needless to say I could not receive him with Mama absent."

"I did see him as I arrived and he didn't look best pleased. You must also feel disappointment."

"It does seem a pity," she confessed. "The day has been exceeding dull up to now. When Lord Mayne was paying court to you last year, I confess I wondered what caused you to throw your cap over the windmill, but he has such charm and address I can readily understand it the better now."

It was much as Valentina feared and as she sought to find the right words to say to her sister, Daphne's radiant expression faded a little.

"Those rumours of late about you and Stockdale were not of my doing, Valentina. I have not breathed a word to anyone of what you told me."

"I know," Valentina answered, casting her a reassuring smile. "The blame for it lies elsewhere."

The girl looked happier then. "Your apparent felicity has dispelled the rumours and I have been so pleased to see you and Stockdale together and in such accord." She looked suddenly doubtful. "It is not . . . merely to dispel the rumours, is it, Valentina?"

She averted her eyes before saying in a muted tone, "I am afraid so."

"Oh no! Oh, Val, you are a chuckle-head! I did so hope you would in time come to appreciate the worth of the man you married."

Valentina turned then to give her sister a smile. "Nothing has changed, my dear."

"You are . . . not still enamoured of Lord Mayne . . . ?"

Valentina threw back her head and laughed. "La! What a notion. You need have no fear on that score, my dear. I have seen Lord Mayne for what he really is, and can only regret that I once encouraged him."

Daphne, however, continued to look uneasy. "You relieve me, for as you know he has been in earnest over me for some time."

"That is of no account. It is your regard for him which really matters. Do you hold him in high esteem, Daphne?"

"Well, he is, of course, so handsome," she enthused, "and with such address. One cannot help but favour him above all others."

Irritated, Valentina retorted, "If Papa would not accept him on my behalf, he would not consider him for you."

"'Tis not the same," she replied, her eyes wide. "After all, let us speak plain, my love; you are a beauty as well as an heiress and Papa would have been failing in his duty if he had not secured the best possible match for you. Our parents cannot expect such a brilliant match for me. I have neither your looks nor address."

"You deride yourself needlessly," Valentina replied, feeling helpless in the face of her sister's apparent devotion to this man. "You are very well-favoured and I am not the only person to think so."

"You are too kind, but all the same a viscount might well be very welcome to Papa, and I cannot see any barrier if you no longer love him."

Unable to bear the thought any longer Valentina jumped to her feet and rushed across the room to sit by her sister's side, taking one of Daphne's hands in hers. She entirely abandoned all caution and tact.

"Oh, do not, I beg of you, consider his offer, Daphne! He is a fortune hunter who will take your portion and dissipate it, leaving you desolate. He is cold and mercenary, and like to break your heart."

"You cannot possibly mean that you now believe Papa was correct in not accepting his offer to you?" Daphne asked in amazement.

Valentina was forced to avert her eyes. "In not accepting Lord Mayne's offer, I own he was quite correct."

Daphne continued to stare at her. "You always spoke so well of Lord Mayne. He was always beyond compare."

"That was before I knew his full measure. He is not the man I believed him to be. Oh, believe me, dearest, I have no wish to distress you, but I know he has been dangling after an heiress for an age."

"So do many men."

Valentina gasped with exasperation. "You must heed me! I know him better than you, Daphne. He will not make you happy!"

Daphne smiled, not at all perturbed by her sister's dire warnings. "*You* would not heed anyone's advice."

"Oh, Daphne, I am totally out of patience with you. You know I wish only for your future happiness."

"You must think my head is filled with goose-feathers. Of course I know Oliver Mayne is dangling after my fortune, just as he coveted yours and a dozen others. I have no intention of accepting his offer and neither has Papa!"

Valentina drew back then; it was her

turn to display total astonishment. "Then why...? You have done nought but encourage him since you came out."

"It serves him right. I have been rather wicked, Val, for I merely wanted you to see him as he really is, and now you have I shall have no more to do with him."

Valentina continued to stare at her sister before a half smile crossed her face. "Daphne, you are indeed a wicked, wicked creature. Why, you've been leading him by the nose for all this time!"

"Only so that you should not throw away a good marriage on his behalf."

A lump began to form in Valentina's throat and tears pricked at her eyes.

"You need have no fear. Lord Mayne has no place in my future plans."

"Then," her sister asked hesitantly, "you are reconciled at last to your marriage?"

"No. It is too late for that now, but it is very important to me that you should be happy."

They hugged each other for some time before a footman arrived to announce a caller, one of Daphne's more favoured suitors.

"Shall I receive him?" she asked anxiously.

Valentina was in a gay mood now and she laughed. "Of course. Whilst I am here, why not?"

They exchanged conspiratorial looks and then Valentina gave the order for the young man to be shown up. When he was shown into the drawing room a few minutes later he was taken aback to discover the two young ladies laughing merrily together.

Ten

Valentina returned to Stockdale House in high spirits only to find herself summoned immediately to the library. As she removed her snow-speckled pelisse some of her good spirits immediately evaporated, but until she was free of him she acknowledged she must bend to his will.

One of the footmen thrust open the library door for her and she was met by the warmth of the fire which was roaring up the chimney. She was surprised, however, to find a stranger with the marquis. Valentina looked from one to the other as her husband came forward. The stranger had been in the course of eating a hearty meal on the marquis's desk and consuming the cold collation as if he had never eaten before.

"Ah, my dear, you are here at last. I trust that the inclement weather did not delay you."

Still gazing at the newcomer, she answered absently, "Hardly at all. I have only been at Mount Street bearing my sister company."

"Well, allow me to introduce my old friend, the Comte de Fontaine."

The Frenchman immediately stopped eating and quickly wiped his hands and lips on a napkin. He pushed the chair back and got to his feet, staring at her all the time.

He was, she was forced to admit, extremely handsome, with fair hair and dark blue eyes which she suspected would in normal circumstances sparkle. But his eyes were full of despair and he was unnaturally thin beneath his shabby clothes. In one place his coat was torn to reveal the lining beneath.

Valentina could not imagine how the Revolution had happened. It seemed inconceivable that their own servants should turn against them, and yet it had happened in France with frightful consequences. Involuntarily she shuddered.

"Monsieur," she said at last, when she had recovered, "welcome to England and to Stockdale House."

He took her hand almost as eagerly as he devoured the food and raised it to his lips.

"Madame, madame, I am most grateful to be here and to make your acquaintance at last."

"Monsieur de Fontaine has not eaten a proper meal in more than a sen'night," the marquis told her. "He has had to wait in hiding until he could find a boat which was willing to bring him to England."

Valentina's eyes doubled with pain. "How you have suffered, monsieur. Be assured we shall do everything in our power to make you comfortable here, and you must regard this as your home for as long as you wish."

The comte let her hand go and looked at his friend. "She is an angel, Stockdale." He looked at Valentina again and her cheeks grew pink at such fulsome praise, especially in view of her earlier reluctance to have him there. "My dear friend, *le mar-*

quis, has always had exquisite taste in all things, but in choosing you as his bride he has surpassed himself. He is the luckiest man alive."

The marquis listened in silence, a wry smile on his face, before he said, "Whatever else you have lost, *mon ami*, you still retain a honeyed tongue."

"Monsieur is very kind," Valentina murmured in embarrassment.

For one who was accustomed to extravagant praise, this was effusive indeed and his manner of delivering a compliment was devastating.

"How can you allow such a divine creature out of your sight for a moment?" asked the comte. "Are there not a score of men waiting to seduce her?"

"More like a hundred," answered the marquis wryly, "but my wife is very circumspect."

"Then you are doubly blessed."

All the time the exchange was taking place, Valentina kept her eyes averted. She couldn't help but be flattered by the Frenchman's regard.

"Have you had enough to eat?" she asked quickly, mindful of his deprivations.

He laughed. "*Mais oui*, more than enough for now, madame."

"You must strive to keep warm," she went on, still flustered by his regard. "The weather is treacherous and I'm persuaded you have been exposed to the worst of it."

For the first time his eyes twinkled and he showed a vestige of his normal rakish self. "I shall enjoy being cossetted by you, madame."

"You have had an eventful time of late," the marquis conceded. "Mayhap, if you have eaten your fill, you had best rest for a while and try to regain your spirits."

"Ah, a clean bed and safety. It is most welcome."

"When my tailor comes I shall send him up to you immediately."

The comte cast a woeful look at Valentina. "I do not always look so shabby, madame."

The marquis ushered him towards the door, rather hastily, saying, "A servant will show you to your room, and do not hesitate to ask for anything you wish."

The comte paused by the door to look at Valentina again. "I shall count the minutes until I set eyes upon you again, madame."

She sketched a curtsey and when he had gone the marquis came back to her, saying darkly, "He has gone through hell. We must do all we can to divert him."

"I shall certainly do all I can," she vowed and she was rewarded by the tightest of smiles from her husband. After a moment she went on, "I am so sorry I behaved selfishly when you first mentioned the matter to me."

"Oh, I am certain you are."

"As far as I am concerned I meant what I said in that he can stay here as long as he pleases."

The marquis walked across to the window to stare out at the falling snow. "I am quite certain that you do, my dear, now you have met him." She looked at him curiously as he went on, "My old friend never fails to have a devastating effect upon all females he encounters." He turned on his heel to face her again, his face uncompromisingly grim. "I do not think he will remain all that long after all." Valentina continued to look at him curiously. "He is short of ready cash but that can soon be remedied. He may not be able to live as lavishly as he once did but he did contrive to have some of his family valuables sewn into the lining of his coat, so he is not exactly in dire straights."

"Even so he is in need of the support of his friends."

The marquis smiled yet again. "Until he arrived today I had quite forgotten how devastating his charm can be. In Paris he was notorious for the number of ladies he managed to seduce. I believe, in the circumstances, Valentina, it would be unwise for him to remain here above the necessary."

She gasped and drew back when she realised his meaning. "You are insulting, Stockdale. Do you really believe I would fall for his flummery?"

"If you do," he answered in a bored voice, "you would not be amongst the first several hundred."

He turned away, picking up a chicken leg which the comte had not eaten and biting into it.

Valentina's heart filled with fury. "You must think me crack-brained indeed. First you consider me selfish for not wanting him here, and now you accuse me of flirting with him."

"As I told you, many level-headed chits have found de Fontaine's charm irresistible. You can hardly claim devotion to me as an excuse to resist him."

Her eyes narrowed but then she threw back her head proudly. "Then beware of any man who comes close to me, for I am like to take him as a lover! Since I am like to be such a troublesome creature I only wonder that you dared to take me as your wife."

All through her castigation he had continued to eat the chicken unconcernedly, which did nothing to ease her anger. At last he put it down and, taking up a clean napkin, proceeded to wipe his hands and lips unhurriedly.

"Why *did* you marry me?" she asked at last.

He glanced at her quickly and away again. "You choose to forget my declaration of devotion which I made to you on our betrothal, so I suggest you tell me my reason."

Valentina howled with anger. "Oh I know it, make no mistake. This divorce will suit you very well indeed!"

Her breast was heaving with the greatest anger she had ever experienced but he

remained unmoved, a further spur to her
fury.

"How can you say such a thing? It was
your unwillingness to become a true and
dutiful wife which prompted my offer in the
first place, one you accepted with the greatest alacrity."

Acknowledging that it was probably
what he had planned all along and she had
foolishly fallen into his trap, caused her
nothing but impotent rage which almost
choked her.

Unable to gainsay his logic, Valentina
turned and rushed to the door. Her skirt,
however, became entangled in the heel of
her shoe and she fell headlong to the ground.

The marquis was immediately there to
help her up. Tears of self-pity were already
streaking her face as she attempted to
straighten her curls and then her velvet
skirts. Ungraciously she did not acknowledge his assistance but when she turned to
go again he retained her hand in his.

"Valentina, you talk as if you wish it
were not so. I am wrong, am I not?"

She stared at him in alarm and astonishment and when she didn't answer he
pulled her closer, causing some alarm. Sud-

denly she realised that he had retained his hold on her and tried to move away, without success.

"Unhand me, Stockdale," she pleaded, twisting her hand in an attempt to prise it free from his grasp.

"Not until I have an answer."

Angry again at his repeated humiliations she cried, "This is my answer," and sank her teeth into his hand.

An explosion of oaths filled the air and she ran to the door. He caught her again, pulling her close.

She tried to free herself again, fearing that she had goaded him too far even though, she reasoned, he had baited her. His face was a mask of fury, his eyes glittered with malice as he drew her close to him so that scarcely an inch was between them. It frightened her to realise he probably hated her as much as she had once declared she loathed him.

"I should like to tame you," he said through clenched teeth. "You have had your way too long, madame, and I have a mind to teach you who is the master here."

Her heart was beating so fast she could hardly breathe and then, miraculously, he let her go, thrusting her back so violently she fell against the door.

"Get out of my sight!" he spat.

As he turned his back on her and walked away, Valentina, her eyes still wide with fear, fumbled with the door handle until it gave way and she stumbled out into the hall.

The sound of hooves on the gravel in front of the house brought Valentina back to wakefulness. Immediately she recalled the ugly scene which had been enacted a few hours earlier and, groaning, she sank back into the pillows longing for the forgetfulness of sleep again.

She realised how foolish she had been and yet he had goaded her, perhaps deliberately. It was no excuse; they had contrived for months to live together with a degree of equanimity and now it was all ended. She regretted that.

Suddenly she realised she had fallen asleep fully dressed, her hat discarded carelessly on a table where she had thrown it in a gesture of despair. The light was fading fast, the fire burning low in the grate, and yet she made no move to summon her maid.

The door opened and after glancing carefully inside, Mary came in bearing a jug of hot water.

"I've been in once, m'lady," she explained, "only you were so fast asleep I didn't want to disturb you. Such a to-do in the house with the poor French gentleman, but he's set many a heart racing below stairs I can tell you. Giggling and sniggering knows no end, and they're all fighting for the honour of serving him."

Mary chattered on, heedless of Valentina's silence, as she quickly went round the room, lighting sconces and candelabra. When she crossed to the window she gave her mistress a critical look at last.

"Ma'am, are you feeling unwell?"

"Just a headache, Mary, but I really look so hag-ridden I had best cry off dinner with the Altons tonight."

"I shall see that his lordship is informed, and then I'm going to bring up a nice possett."

As Valentina wondered how she could ever face him again with any degree of composure, Mary reached up to close the curtains. As she did so she said, "Now, I wonder who'd be calling at this time of the day?"

Valentina was on her feet then, peering down on to the carriage drive and gasped as she drew back as if stung.

"It is my mother-in-law's carriage. What in heaven's name has brought her from Tunbridge?"

She stood almost motionless for a few stunned seconds before becoming animated. "Mary, ring for a servant." As the girl hurried to do so she went on, "I must have the tapestry chair brought down from the attics. If it is not in the drawing room she will never forgive me. It should never have been removed."

"Get me out of this gown and into the dun brocade, and then bring out my sapphires and diamonds, Mary."

"You have the headache, ma'am," the maid reminded her as she returned from the bell pull to unhook Valentina's crumpled gown.

"That is no excuse. If I cry off the dowager will most certainly deeem me a sickly creature and assume this is a regular occurrence when I never suffer from the headache at all."

She peered worriedly into the full length mirror. "Oh, I do look a sight! You must tidy my hair, Mary, and put some rouge on my cheeks even though I fear it will be to no avail. Oh, do hurry!"

The day had been one of the most trying she could ever remember and now the arrival of her mother-in-law filled her with dread as she steeled herself for the eventual encounter.

Much to Valentina's relief when she went downstairs she found the dowager marchioness safely ensconced in the tapestry chair, and she vowed to herself never to move it again.

As she came down the stairs a glance in the mirrors which lined the walls assured her that there were no telltale signs to ravage her appearance.

She entered the drawing room experiencing a great deal of apprehension, and it transpired it was worse than she had anticipated, for the Comte de Fontaine was also present. His appearance, however, had improved since the afternoon. He looked more rested and it appeared that the marquis's tailor had contrived to provide him with a splendid velvet evening coat.

When she paused in the doorway the

comte's eyes surveyed her frankly and with pleasure, but Valentina's attention was taken by her husband to whom she immediately looked.

He had changed his clothes, too, and was wearing evening dress, and for the first time she realised that although he did not possess conventional good looks, he was, nevertheless, an imposing man.

He ignored her and Valentina wasn't certain whether she was relieved or chagrined. It was left to the comte to escort her in.

"You look *magnifique*," he said in a low voice.

"And you look far better than you did this afternoon," she responded.

"So here you are at last!" her mother-in-law's voice boomed out across the room.

Valentina curtseyed and then kissed the painted cheek which was liberally adorned with black patches.

"I am heartily sorry I was not here to greet you when you arrived, my lady."

"Stockdale informed me that you were resting. I trust you are quite well?"

"Perfectly." As she drew away she said breathlessly, "Your arrival was a surprise indeed. Stockdale was most remiss in not telling me of your coming."

"He did not know."

"Then what turn of fortune has caused you to honour us so unexpectedly, ma'am?"

The dowager's lips were pressed firmly together in a disapproving line.

"Mama has heard some ridiculous rumour that all is not well between us," the marquis said, breaking his silence at last as he handed his mother a glass of ratafia.

As the dowager lived out of London, Valentina was taken aback to discover she had heard the rumours. She glanced fearfully at her husband who was taking a pinch of snuff and affecting unconcern. Following his example, she fluttered her fan and laughed light-heartedly.

"La! How foolish that is. Someone must be jealous of our felicity."

"So I have told Mama," the marquis added, giving her a cool look which spelled out his displeasure very clearly.

"I am relieved, however, to hear that all is well," the dowager conceded, sipping at the ratafia. "As you can imagine I was somewhat distressed. Others must do as they please, but never a breath of scandal has ever touched the Stockdales, and I pray that it never will."

"*Mon dieu!*" exclaimed the comte. "This slur is infamous. I would kill the man who had slandered me."

"Rest assured," the marquis answered in a cold voice which sent shivers down his wife's spine, "I shall do so when I discover who the scoundrel is."

Valentina walked a few paces across the room. "What a pity you were obliged to travel so far to receive reassurance, Lady Stockdale, especially as you hate coming to Town so heartily. We shall have to ensure you are able to return home as soon as possible."

The dowager laughed gruffly. "Would it were possible." Valentina stared at her, aware that for the first time the marquis was smiling. "This is all your fault, you naughty boy," she said to the Frenchman and her daughter-in-law was amazed at the softness which had crept into her voice when she addressed the comte.

It seemed that even she was not immune to his charms.

"My fault, madame? How can that be?"

"I cannot be the only one to have heard

this foolish tattle, and if you, dear Jacques, are to be here in this house it might give rise to even more talk—this time, perchance, of a *ménage à trois.*"

The comte's eyebrows rose a fraction, the marquis turned away, still smiling, and Valentina started violently.

"Such gossip will never begin if *I* am here," her mother-in-law added, bestowing a complacent smile upon them all.

Monsieur de Fontaine looked at Valentina and shrugged apologetically. For his own reasons he was as sorry as she and she knew then that her husband had not exaggerated about this man.

Quietly the marquis said, "You are very welcome to stay, Mama, for as long as you please."

She cast him a fond, and rare, smile. "I know that very well, my dear."

Rather uncertainly Valentina added, feeling the necessity to say something, "It will be good to have the house full of people."

"My dear," her mother-in-law murmured, "it should be filled with children."

Valentina froze with mortification but then the dowager demanded, "Stockdale, what have you done to your hand?"

Valentina turned on her heel to see that the place she had bitten was now covered with court plaster, and she held her breath as he glowered at her across the room.

"I was attacked by an over-excited animal, Mama," he answered at last.

"Such animals must be dealt with severely," she told him.

"This one will be, I promise you."

When a lackey entered to announce the arrival of Miss Woodville, Valentina was vastly relieved at the interruption, saying, as her husband gave her a questioning look, "I quite forgot about Daphne in all the excitement of Lady Stockdale's arrival. La! She will be so pleased to see you here. Mama is indisposed and I did promise to chaperon my sister."

"I hope Lady Woodville is not seriously indisposed," said the dowager.

"A headache only," Valentina assured her, "but my sister is most anxious not to miss any diversion."

The comte got to his feet. "Your sister? *Mon dieu!* Is it possible there is another one of you?"

Valentina's manner brightened then. "Indeed, and she is not yet spoken for!"

Daphne hurried in but then she drew back at the sight of so many unexpected faces in the room. Her eyes opened wide when she saw the dowager marchioness but then she sank into a deep curtsey.

"Lady Stockdale, I am honoured."

"It is good to see you again, child. I heard that your debut has been a great success."

She blushed at being thus addressed by so imposing a lady. "Yes, my lady; I have scarce stopped to draw breath since it began."

For once the dowager deemed to smile. "I recall my own well; I could not for anything go through it again. How say you, Valentina?"

"I entirely agree with you, my lady."

In the meantime Daphne's attention had strayed to the comte and Valentina said quickly, "Daphne, my dear, allow me to introduce Monsieur, the comte de Fontaine, recently arrived from Paris."

Daphne's eyes became almost as large as saucers before her expression softened. "Monsieur," she murmured as she sank into a deep curtsey.

The comte took her hand and raised it

to his lips. "Mademoiselle, I am enchanted. Had I known such beauty existed on this side of the Channel I would not have waited for the Revolution to make it necessary for me to come here."

The girl's cheeks flooded with colour and she looked positively beguiled. Valentina could scarcely stop herself rubbing her hands together with satisfaction, for there was no doubt the Frenchman had won a heart even if he had lost everything else.

Eleven

"Is not monsieur le comte the most wonderful man you have ever met?" Daphne asked one evening some weeks later as she and her sister were on their way to Covent Garden.

Valentina smiled. "If I agree you will only consider me to be in love with him."

Daphne blushed. "Oh, you know very well what I mean."

Valentina laid a gloved hand on her sister's arm. "Indeed I do, and I am so glad you find his company congenial."

"How could anyone fail to do so? His

169

mode of address is superior to anything I have ever encountered before."

"'Tis clear you are in the highest of spirits," her sister replied, eyeing her wryly, for it was something she had known since the moment Daphne clapped eyes on the handsome comte.

"I am afraid, too," the girl confided a moment later.

"I can recognise that also. Feeling as you do can be quite alarming."

"I am not afraid of loving him, Val. I am merely afraid that he is not in earnest about me."

"He has been showing a marked partiality towards you of late."

Daphne's eyes gleamed. "He is charming to everyone as you must have noticed, and so many others flirt with him. He is not the greatest catch, but he would be well-received by many." She paused before going on, "I suggested that you and I travel to the opera together so we could have a coze on this very subject. Valentina, he is living beneath your roof. Surely you are in a position to know who, if anyone, he happens to favour."

Her sister stared at her fingers. "He

may be residing at Piccadilly, but in truth I see very little of him. On those occasions when I have he has not made mention of any partiality and, Daphne, I am bound to tell you I cannot discuss such a matter with him."

Daphne sighed. "Yes, I do understand."

"No, you do not. When Monsieur de Fontaine arrived, my husband gave me due warning that he was like to attempt to seduce me and he as much as said he expected the comte to be successful!"

Daphne stared at her in astonishment. "I cannot conceive that Lord Stockdale would be so crack-brained."

"He has no reason to believe me virtuous."

"Lord Stockdale is jealous, more like."

"No, he is not," Valentina answered sadly. "He has an excess of pride which will not allow me to consort with any gentleman whilst we are still wed."

"It all sounds exceeding queer to me. I'd have thought, in the circumstances, he would not care."

"Well, at least you can appreciate I must avoid any personal conversation with the comte."

Wryly, Daphne answered, "If Stockdale is not jealous, I most certainly am, so 'tis just as well. It was my fear you would fall into his arms and that he might fall in love with you, too. You do tend to make a man's head giddy."

"I have given him no encouragement, nor am I like to do so. The truth is that no man finds favour in my eyes. I am sadly disillusioned with the lot of them."

Daphne gazed at her sister's sad profile as the carriage slowed near the opera house. "You know, I would be much happier about Monsieur de Fontaine if I knew you were settled. This business between you and Stockdale is troubling my head a good deal."

Valentina gave her a fond smile. "It is enough that you are happy, Daphne, and I pray the comte is in earnest. Even a rake such as he must settle down to matrimony at some time, and the fact that he has lost his home may make him anxious to establish a new one here."

"We shall have to wait and see what happens," she answered philosophically and then, "Lady Stockdale shows no inclination to depart the Town."

Valentina chuckled then. "She declares

she detests the Season, but since she came to stay she has had more engagements than I."

"Does she not display any inclination to go back to her home in Tunbridge?"

Valentina sighed and rested her head back on the squabs as they waited their turn to drive up to the opera house. "I do not suppose she will go until the Season ends. She declares she has not enjoyed herself so much in years; since before she was widowed in fact, which I do not doubt. But I suspect her real reason is to make absolutely certain those rumours are not true about our marriage."

Daphne cast her an agonised look before saying in a bright tone, "Lady Stockdale seemed so alarming to me at first, but I must own she has been exceeding condescending."

"She is quite a dear beneath that toplofty exterior."

The carriage moved under the portico at last and the two young ladies prepared to climb down. The opera house was already overflowing with ladies richly gowned and bejewelled, accompanied by gentlemen whose finery rivalled that of their partners.

Through the carriage window Valentina espied her mother-in-law, resplendent in purple lustring, huge diamonds about her throat and wrists. She was in earnest conversation with Lady Woodville and a few of their cronies and as was usual dominating all that was said.

Waiting under the portico were the marquis and the comte. Without a word, the marquis handed down his wife and then his sister-in-law. With her cheeks pink and her eyes bright Daphne allowed the comte to accompany her into the opera house and Valentina noted he was very attentive to her. She paused for a moment to stare after them, her eyes misty.

As if reading her mind the marquis said, "They make a handsome pair, do they not?"

Since the day of the comte's arrival they had scarce exchanged a word beyond what was civil or necessary. At the sound of his voice she cast him a cold look, fearing his sarcasm which she had learned could be biting.

A moment later she swallowed her pride and asked, "Stockdale, do you know if he is in earnest?"

He began to lead her inside. "I believe Monsieur de Fontaine is too concerned about the fate of his family to be in earnest about anyone else at present."

"That is a pity, for I fear my sister has thrown her cap over the windmill at last."

The marquis drew in an almost indiscernible sigh. "Then if he does make an offer and it is accepted, he will be the most fortunate of men. Her devotion is assured."

She gave him a sharp look as they approached the others in the party but as she did so he smiled urbanely. "Well, it seems I am in the happy position of escorting four of the loveliest ladies in the land."

"You are not alone in that," the comte pointed out. "I must demand to share the honour."

"Thirty years ago," the dowager responded, not displeased, "you would have been quite correct about me. In fact, you would not have had a chance to get so close to me."

"Oh, you are a pair of toadies," Lady Woodville cried, laughing loudly, "but pray continue to grease my boots as often as you please."

The others laughed and if anyone noticed that Valentina was a trifle more subdued than usual no one commented.

"I think we should take our seats," she pointed out at last.

"An excellent suggestion," agreed the dowager. "You and Miss Woodville took an unconscionable time to arrive."

"I am sorry if you were kept waiting, Lady Stockdale. There is a deal of traffic on the approach to the Piazza."

"Tush!" she retorted, tapping Valentina's arm with her fan. "You and Miss Woodville are prattle-boxes and there is no need for you to gainsay me, for when I was your age I had a sister of my own and there was no bounds to our chattering whenever we were together."

Valentina smiled faintly as they entered the marquis's own box. Boxes on all sides of them were filled with acquaintances to whom they all waved and smiled as they settled into their chairs.

Just before the opera began the Prince of Wales, accompanied by Lady Jersey, arrived with a party of friends and courtiers which made the evening even more exciting for all those present.

On a previous encounter with the Prince

of Wales, Valentina had found him charming and extremely handsome. However, Lady Stockdale was not entranced by him.

"He is nought but a popinjay," she declared, "even though he no longer claims to be married to Maria Fitzherbert. Lady Jersey, it seems, is his favourite now and how she basks in the glory of it."

The countess, reputed to be the Prince's latest mistress, did indeed look proud as she acknowledged friends and acquaintances on all sides.

Then Lady Woodville said, "Were you not once Her Majesty's lady-in-waiting?"

Valentina looked at her mother-in-law in amazement. "I had no notion of that, my lady."

"The court was exceeding dull," the dowager answered. "No doubt it still is except that the King's illness, which thankfully is over now, will have livened it up, no doubt. Her Majesty must be a very worried woman. The Prince as Regent would be a disaster this country can do without, and she would know it better than any of us." She glared then at the marquis, "My son is remiss in not telling you of something of so much import."

At this point he leaned forward. "My wife and I are still to be considered newlyweds and, as such, in the process of getting to know each other better."

Valentina turned away in confusion, aware that all eyes had turned on her and the expression in her husband's was more than a little malicious.

Later, as she glanced around the box, she reflected that it was a satisfactory state of affairs—almost exclusively a family occasion. It caused her no small feeling of sadness, too, for she knew it was a sham. Her own emotions were a mystery to her; she only knew she was no longer elated by the prospect of being free of the man she had married. The knowledge had been slow in coming to her and it was a revelation she wished she did not have to face.

When the interval came, everyone remained in their boxes until the Royal party had left.

"That was quite splendid!" exclaimed Lady Woodville. "I declare I do not know when I have enjoyed a performance more."

"It would be an improvement if those young fools in the pit would refrain from calling out to the ladies," the dowager answered in a censorious voice which immediately dampened Lady Woodville's enthusiasm.

The marquis smiled. "Mama, it has never been any different and I fear it never will."

The dowager and Lady Woodville led the party out of the box, Lady Stockdale saying, "I thought His Highness looked a trifle peaked tonight."

"'Tis no wonder, Mama," her son replied. "Young Florizel has always burned the candle at both ends. I could never keep up with him."

"That is saying something!" she answered with a laugh.

Then the marquis took Valentina's arm in a tight grip, much to her alarm. "His Highness should venture into matrimony. It would be the salvation of him, to be sure."

The others laughed but Lady Woodville looked smug. Valentina could only feel vexed, knowing he was mocking her once more.

When they were accosted by countless friends and acquaintances her mind was diverted for a while until she realised that there was no sign of her husband. As she attempted to converse with an old admirer she continually looked for a sight of him, and finally did so. Through the milling crowds she saw him pull back the curtain to one of the boxes and then go inside.

Intrigued, she excused herself and followed, even though her passage was barred by many eager to engage her in conversation. At last she reached the spot where she had seen him and attempted to discover who else was inside that particular box. Because of the noise of conversation in the lobby she was obliged to move closer than she really wished, and then all caution was lost for she stiffened with indignation when she recognised the voice of Lady Goodhayes.

"I am not at all happy about this," Valentina heard her say. "It is not as I thought it would be."

"Don't fly into a pucker, my dear. It is going just as it should. We have seen so little of each other of late there could not possibly be a whisper of gossip."

"Not seeing you is what I am most unhappy about," she replied and Valentina choked back a gasp of vexation.

"Ah, but only think, by the end of the Season all the pretence will be over."

"I cannot conceive that this will really come right in the end, Stockdale."

"It will," he answered in soothing tones, "I promise that it will. By the end of the Season all will be wonderful and I shall be the happiest of men."

"But it is so long," she protested. "How can you bear it, for I cannot."

"I can bear any manner of hardship if it means the future holds its promise."

"Oh, it will. Yes, I am sure that it will. You have been so brave and so true, it is only just you should achieve your heart's desire."

Valentina's hands flew to her lips to stifle a cry of anguish which threatened to escape them. Shaking, she almost stumbled away from the box.

Of course, she had known about her husband's relationship with Lady Goodhayes, but to hear them actually conspiring together filled her with pain and rage.

She was, however, not to be allowed privacy to recover her composure, for as she blindly moved away from the box a voice said, "Lady Stockdale. It is Lady Stockdale, is it not?"

She turned around in alarm to come

face to face with the portly figure of the Prince of Wales himself, the garter star pinned to the wide expanse of his evening coat.

"Your Highness," she gasped, sinking into a deep curtsey, for her mind was still occupied with what she had heard pass between her husband and Lady Goodhayes.

"I thought it was you when I quizzed the boxes," he continued. "Did I not say so, Alvanley?"

The man at his side smiled faintly. "Indeed you did, sir."

"Your Highness's memory is exceptional," Valentina told him in a breathless voice.

"It is always that where a beautiful woman is concerned. The ugly ones I forget immediately."

Her cheeks grew pink, aware that the encounter was being observed and commented upon by many.

"I hope," he went on a moment later, "you will do me the honour of attending my next soirée at Carlton House."

"It is I who would be most honoured, sir," she replied, her mind still in a whirl.

"Good. My equerry will send you an invitation. Carlton House needs must be decorated with beautiful woman, and if I, the Prince of Wales, cannot insist upon that, who can, eh?"

He laughed and all those within earshot did so, too. As he and Lord Alvanley walked away, Valentina curtseyed again.

When she began to fan herself furiously her momentary glory and pleasure evaporated. The Prince may have paid her an enormous compliment, but to be discarded unwanted by one's husband must be the greatest humiliation, and one she was certain she would never survive.

"Lady Stockdale." Again she turned, this time to come face to face with someone she did not want to see. "It seems that in the future, with Royal patronage, you will not be without influence. I had no notion you were so ambitious. How foolish of me to believe you might once have been interested in so minor a member of the nobility such as I happen to be."

She averted her face, not even troubling to counter his distasteful innuendoes. "Lord Mayne, I was not aware of your presence this evening."

He swayed unsteadily in front of her

and his lips twisted into a sneer. "That does not surprise me, ma'am. I only wonder you recall my name."

Valentina affected a laugh, realising that the viscount was in an ugly mood and from what she could perceive he was foxed, too.

"I could scarce forget someone so ill-mannered," she replied, turning to walk away, but he put his hand on her arm to stay her.

"I want to talk to you."

She glanced scathingly at his importuning hand before answering, "I don't believe we have anything to say to one another."

"Well I certainly have something to say to you. Miss Woodville has, of late, refused to receive me and only just now has snubbed me in full view of everyone."

"She has an excess of good sense."

"As she once received my calls with alacrity, I can only assume it is you who have caused this change in her."

Once again Valentina laughed and if it was a forced one, she was certain no one could guess.

"Lord Mayne, I have no influence over

my sister's emotions. She is free to do as she pleases. You must be aware that a lady's fancy is always capricious. In fact, there are many gentlemen who are almost as changeable in their affections."

His eyes darkened almost to black and his cheeks grew red. "So that is the way of it; a woman scorned."

"I don't know what you may mean, Lord Mayne. This is all a nonsense."

As Valentina glared at him, feeling nothing but contempt, she wondered that she had ever believed herself in love with such a shallow creature.

"Oh, I harbour no doubts that it is you who have done this. Now she is favouring that penniless Frenchie."

"I can assure you that Monsieur de Fontaine is far from penniless, Lord Mayne, and again I say let go of my arm."

"No! Not until I have had my say. It is your influence which has spoiled my chances and you will be very sorry for it, I promise you."

"Mayne, my wife has made a very reasonable request. Be pleased to unhand her."

He did so with alacrity on hearing the icy tones of Lord Stockdale who sauntered up to them with Daphne and the comte. The sight of them, however, only served to fuel the viscount's drunken anger.

"Your *wife*," he growled. "Your wife indeed. The entire world will soon know how much of a wife she is!"

From indolence, the marquis's manner changed almost imperceptibly to one of quiet fury. As Valentina watched the scene fearfully her heart began to beat fast with trepidation. In his drunken state Lord Mayne was no match for the marquis.

"Your manner offends me, Mayne, but this matter cannot be settled here. My seconds will call upon you first thing in the morning."

Both Valentina and her sister gasped, and Lord Mayne, as if struck, staggered backwards. "There is no need..."

"You have insulted not only me, but my wife who has made it plain she wants no more to do with you."

"I beg your pardon most heartily," he stammered, and Valentina felt even more contemptuous to see him so craven. "I meant no offence, my...lord. Such drastic action will not...be necessary."

The marquis stepped forward, causing

the other man to flinch away. "Very well. Your apology is accepted—this time—but you will not escape so easily if I ever catch you talking to my wife again."

He stumbled away into the crowds and Valentina drew a sigh of relief that there would be no confrontation after all. The marquis watched him go until he was lost in the crowds. A silence had descended upon the lobby during the argument but now an excited chattering started up again.

"He is an unlicked cub," the comte remarked in outraged tones.

"Just one of my wife's disappointed suitors," the marquis informed him in a pleasant voice, although the look which raked Valentina was far from kindly.

"There must be a score of them," the comte replied.

"Let us return to the box," Lady Woodville suggested as she breezed past, evidently unaware of the strained atmosphere. "I hear the music starting up."

"What an excellent idea," the marquis responded, giving Valentina his arm which she took, albeit reluctantly.

"The interval," commented the comte,

"has been almost as interesting as the opera performance!"

A comment which elicited a great deal of laughter from everyone except Valentina who remained quiet and thoughtful throughout the rest of the evening.

Twelve

The mercer's assistant took down a bolt of cloth to join several others lying on the counter.

"This lustring will become you well well, Lady Stockdale. It has only just arrived on a ship which docked yesterday."

Valentina fingered it doubtfully as Daphne agreed. "It is very fine, Valentina. All of them are."

The assistant turned to bring down yet another bolt. His eyes gleamed with anticipation. "Figured muslin, my lady. The very latest thing from the Indies!"

"It seems a trifle light," Valentina answered, fingering it with no enthusiasm."

"Ah, but it will soon be all the crack. A leader of fashion such as yourself, my lady, needs must be ahead of all others and I have not offered this particular cloth to anyone else as yet."

She glanced at her sister. "Very well. Have it sent to Lady Woodville." Daphne gave her a curious look as Valentina turned away from the counter and pulled on her gloves. "It will be of more use to you, Daphne. I have enough gowns for the remainder of the Season, and then..."

Her voice trailed away and she began to walk towards the door. Daphne hurried to catch up with her. "Do you know what Jacques told me the other evening?"

Valentina paused to cast her a withering look. "Jacques?"

Daphne blushed. "Monsieur de Fontaine." Then she went on, eager again. "He said no man would challenge a man to duel over a woman he did not love to distraction."

"You didn't discuss Stockdale and me with him!"

"No, of course, I didn't; what he said

was 'Stockdale must be quite lost for love to call Lord Mayne out.'"

Valentina continued to fasten her gloves calmly and with no outward reaction to this comment. "A man will fight over any slight to his pride, Daphne, and he is an exceeding proud man."

"No one can have more excessive pride than you, Val. You will not, even now, admit you no longer dislike Lord Stockdale so heartily."

Valentina could not meet her eyes. "You and I have never been able to hide our true feelings from one another, Daphne. How ironic the situation is, but had I behaved differently from the beginning, I doubt if anything could be changed. My husband's heart belongs to another and his feelings are more constant than mine, I fear."

Her sister gazed at her pityingly. "We are both pitiable creatures in yearning for what we may never have."

"Ah, but hopefully you have a great chance of future happiness. I have dissipated any I might have had. I can blame no one but myself."

"I have heard the most delightful *on dit*," the girl confided a moment later. "One that is certain to cheer you. After Mayne's behaviour at the opera house the other evening, his aunt, who supplies all his funds, sent him to rusticate, so he can repent his foolishness."

At this revelation Valentina could not help but laugh. "That is good news indeed! However, Lord Mayne is gone and forgotten for both of us and what I wish to know is why Papa has not accepted any of the offers of marriage which have been made for you?"

"Because I have asked him not to."

"He never heeded me in that," her sister retorted in hurt tones.

"You refused several before Stockdale came along, and Papa would not turn down the Marquis of Stockdale whatever you said. If such an offer were made for me I don't doubt he would accept it however much I protested that I loved Jacques—Monsieur de Fontaine," she amended as her cheeks flooded with colour.

"It is rare not to find him at your side these days, Daphne," Valentina said as she nodded to an acquaintance.

"Today he is inspecting a house in Manchester Square which might suit him, and I know he daily enquires of newly-arrived emigrés about his family's fate."

Valentina drew a sigh. "'Tis such a sad business. I know the loss of his estates and the silence about his family has sapped his spirit. It's so terrible not to know whether they're alive or dead."

"Mayhap it would be worse if he did know," Daphne replied, similarly downcast. "I long to comfort him."

Valentina smiled sympathetically. "I am persuaded he is exceeding fond of you."

Daphne's answering smile was a brave one as they stepped outside the warehouse and into the Strand where a multitude of carriages were awaiting their noble passengers.

Valentina signalled for her own carriage to approach.

"You are being very brave," Daphne told her. "I am persuaded I should not behave with such admirable spirit."

"It is my admirable spirit which has caused my troubles, but never fear, I shall contrive, my dear. My only concern is that Mama and Lady Stockdale should not suspect anything amiss until the very last moment."

Daphne giggled behind her hand. "Mama has noted your varying moods of late and has come to the conclusion that you must be in a delicate condition."

The notion horrified Valentina but then, philosophically, she decided, "She will soon realise she is wrong."

"Have you ever considered that it may not be too late to begin again?"

"I cannot deny that there have been moments when it may have been possible, but I foolishly did not heed them."

"Could you not confess your mistake to Lord Stockdale, Valentina? Mayhap, there is a chance to begin together as you should."

"Never," her sister vowed. "It would be in vain and I have no mind to make a cake of myself."

She stiffened as a shabby whisky pulled up in front of the emporium and Lady Goodhayes climbed down accompanied by a maidservant and a child of about three years.

Valentina was very tempted to pretend she had not seen them, but when she acknowledged that this was not possible she stared at the child hard, at the same time hating to do so. The sight of him, however, held a morbid fascination.

His hair was as dark as his mother's was fair and Valentina strove to discover a likeness to her husband, but apart from their similar colouring there was none.

"Why, good day to you, Lady Stock-dale," the woman said, somewhat taken aback.

"Good day, Lady Goodhayes. Are you acquainted with my sister, Miss Wood-ville?"

Daphne sketched a curtsey. "How do you do, ma'am?"

Lady Goodhayes managed a more genuine smile towards Daphne; something which Valentina could not help but notice.

"I note that your Season is a great success, Miss Woodville."

"I am enjoying it hugely, ma'am."

"Did you enjoy your evening at the opera last week?" Valentina asked and the woman started slightly.

The fact that Lady Goodhayes invariably acted ill-at-ease in her company did nothing to endear her to Valentina, although she knew in other circumstances she might have been able to make a true friend of this woman.

"Yes, yes indeed," she answered after a moment, feigning amusement. "It was very pleasant, but I had no notion you had seen me there. From all I have heard you were well occupied with admirers."

"But that is true of all of us," she answered sweetly and then, looking at the child who was beginning to show signs of impatience, "This must be your son, of whom I have heard so much."

The woman flushed with pleasure. "I cannot conceive who might have spoken of him."

"Hello, young man," Valentina said to the child.

"Toby," his mother said sharply, "where are your manners?"

The child bowed and Valentina said truthfully, feeling suddenly wistful, "He must be a great comfort to you, Lady Good-hayes."

"Indeed he is. That is why I have his company more often than most mothers. All too soon he will be grown with a family of his own."

"You may yet have another family,

Lady Goodhayes. You are too young to re-main a widow." Before the woman could comment, Valentina went on to ask, "Tell me, does he favour his father?"

She flushed. "I am often told that he does. I've always believed that boys should favour their fathers. Don't you agree? Or perchance you will feel more able to com-ment when you have young ones of your own."

She smiled, as if surprised and pleased at her own pronouncement, and then peer-ing into the emporium, "I do hope they have a new selection today. Did you make some worthwhile purchases, Lady Stockdale?"

"Only on my sister's behalf. I am not in need of anything at present. You, no doubt, will wish for a greater selection of clothes than you have at present."

Lady Goodhayes looked abashed. "I have lived a very quiet life since my hus-band died."

"No doubt that may well change," Val-entina snapped, "if you remarry."

The sisters bade her a quick goodbye and climbed into the waiting barouche.

"I cannot believe that Stockdale is in love with that colourless creature," Daphne declared as the carriage set off along the Strand.

"She will never cause any affront to his pride, nor invite the scandal my mother-in-law fears so much. She is ideal."

"And what shall you do, my dear? I'll warrant you have not considered the matter of late."

Valentina's eyes glittered with a strange intensity. "There will be no lack of suitors, but if the Prince of Wales wishes me to become his mistress I shall do so willingly and use my influence with him to exclude them from Court. That, I fancy," she added with a degree of satisfaction evident in her voice, "will play Old Harry with his damnable pride."

Daphne gazed at her sister in astonishment before saying gently, "Will that ease the pain in your heart, Valentina?"

The marchioness buried her face in her hands and answered in a muffled voice, "No, it will not!"

And for the first time began to sob heartbrokenly on her sister's shoulder.

By the time she arrived back at Piccadilly, Valentina was once more composed. The sparkle in her eyes, although not attributable to pleasure, nevertheless became her well.

"Is Lord Stockdale at home?" she asked immediately, to be told that he was out.

A great many calling cards had been left in her absence, together with the usual number of gifts and flowers sent by gentlemen anxious to solicit her favour.

It wasn't usual for a lady to take a lover before having a child to satisfy the succession, but there were those who could always hope to find favour in her eyes. Some of them she had found attractive in the days before her marriage, but more and more now Valentina imagined what it would be like to be held in the arms of the man she had married. It was a thought which often left her weak with a desire destined never to be satisfied.

The news that the marquis was not at home was both a relief and a disappointment. Valentina wanted to see him and yet dreaded to do so. Since the comte's arrival, the relationship between her and the marquis had steadily worsened and after the scene at Covent Garden he had scarce spoken to her at all.

There was a time when such behaviour would only have pleased her but now she felt her heart was breaking. She was frightened, too. She needed no calendar to tell her the social year was drawing to its close. Her marriage was almost a year old and that was ending, too.

At its beginning Valentina had wanted only her freedom, but a divorced wife was entitled to nothing and she wondered, for the first time, what she would do when she had the freedom which had once seemed so precious. The thought of throwing herself upon her parents' charity was abhorrent to her and even though there were very many men who would be glad enough to set her up in her own establishment and shower her with gifts and jewels, her independent spirit baulked at that. Besides, she could only take as a lover a man to whom she was devoted and she loved only one man.

After she had changed out of her outdoor clothes she went downstairs again, hoping that an acquaintance would call to impart all the latest gossip and thus divert her mind from all its unwelcome thoughts. Even the arrival of the dowager would have been welcome at that moment, but she, as

Valentina knew very well, was with her cronies at a card party.

As she looked over the first floor balcony she was surprised to see the comte arriving at that time of the day. Even more surprising his head was bent, his shoulders sagged and he seemed altogether pitiable as he went into the library.

Because he had seemed in such good spirits of late, Valentina was intrigued and she came quickly down the stairs. When she went inside the library she found him staring down at the desk top as if it were the most fascinating thing in the world. As the door closed, his head snapped up and there was no mistaking the bleak look on his face.

"Monsieur, what is wrong? I fear something is terribly amiss."

"*C'est terrible.* I have heard today that my brother and his family have been tried and executed by the Committee for Public Safety."

Valentina's eyes opened wide with horror and she rushed to comfort him. "Is there no possibility of a mistake?"

"None. I have the news from first hand witnesses who only just escaped with their own lives."

Her eyes grew moist. "Oh, monsieur, what can I say to you?"

"I am desolate even though I am given to believe my youngest brother has been seen alive quite recently."

"You must pray that it is true. I shall." She wrung her hands together in anguish. "Oh, what barbarity and in the name of what cause?"

He covered his face with his hands. "The worst thing is that I know now I shall never go back to France again."

"Don't lose heart," she pleaded. "This madness cannot continue. It must surely end soon."

"I cannot see that, and even if it were so, my chateau is in ruins now, Jean-Pierre is dead, Michel will come to England if he can. It is finished."

Valentina watched him, horror-stricken, and then she hurried to the table where a number of cut glass decanters were standing on a silver tray. With shaking hands she poured a measure of brandy and handed it to him.

"*Merci, merci, jolie madame*," he murmured as he drank it in one gulp and put the glass down.

Valentina continued to watch him anxiously. "Would you have some more, monsieur?"

He shook his head. "How strange it is that brandy is still available here."

"Yes, it can easily be obtained." She hesitated for a moment before saying, "Monsieur—Jacques, you have lost so much it is difficult for you to think of anything else but you must, for the sake of your sanity if for no other reason, and for those who have great regard for you."

He raised his eyes slowly to meet hers and she went on, "You have our deep regard, Jacques—Stockdale's and mine—and you have made many new friends here in London since you arrived. Why not make that your basis for a new beginning?"

"You are so full of kindness and good sense, madame. If it had not been for you and my very good friend, the marquis, I should not have had the will to live after my escape from the *sans culottes*. My lord Stockdale is the most fortunate of men to have taken you for his bride. You are an incredible woman and I admire you greatly."

Valentina was forced to look away from his probing gaze as the comte went on. "I first knew Alexander Stockdale when he was on his Grand Tour. *Mon dieu*, he had the greatest capacity for enjoying life I had ever encountered. He never passed by any of life's pleasures, madame. I knew then that when he eventually married his wife would have to be an exceptional woman, and yet I could not imagine one who possessed so many natural attributes also to be so full of kindness and sensibility. Your husband, madame, is the most fortunate of men and there is only one other who can rival you."

Valentina moved forward then. "Who is that, monsieur?"

"Miss Woodville, naturally."

She was thoughtful. "So you do have regard for her."

"I love her most dearly," he answered in a proud and yet dejected tone.

"And she you," Valentina told him eagerly then. "But why have you not declared yourself?"

"How can I? What can I offer such as she?"

"A great deal, Jacques, and no one is more aware of that than my sister. If you do not come up to scratch soon it will be too late. My father will accept another on her behalf and more unhappiness will be heaped upon what has gone before."

He gave her an anxious look. "Do you really believe I should make an offer for her?"

"Oh yes, Jacques," she implored. "You *must.*"

He smiled at last. "Then I will risk rejection. My pride is of no account any longer. Oh, how can I ever thank you, madame?"

"By being happy," she answered in a husky voice. "Nothing else matters."

To her surprise he caught hold of her hands and kissed her on both cheeks before enfolding her in his arms.

"You have given me hope when I believed all that was left to me was despair. This will be my *renaissance.*"

Valentina laughed as she clung on to him. "A new beginning. Oh yes, indeed. You are so fortunate. Such an opportunity is not open to all."

"What a pretty sight!"

Valentina pulled away from the comte who was also startled and swung round on his heel.

The marquis was standing in the doorway, one hand on the door. His face was a mask of fury at the sight of which Valentina looked afraid and bewildered, but the comte's face grew dark, too, as his friend slammed shut the door behind him.

"How long has this been going on?"

"I don't..." Valentina began to stammer.

"No, do not trouble to tell me. Let me guess instead. Since the day you arrived, my friend."

The comte took a step forward, his entire body bristling with indignation. "You are quite, quite mad, Stockdale!"

"How dare you say that after cuckolding me in my own house. If you had not suffered so greatly I would call you out over this, have no doubt."

"No!" Valentina cried, and received a scathing look from her husband.

The Frenchman laughed harshly. "Oh, do not allow that to stop you, my friend, I would fight you to protect the honour of this lady who, far from being disloyal, is a saint. You are a fool to doubt one so true. If we wished to conduct an *affaire de coeur*, we should be more discreet about it, I assure you. Your wife, with her good sense, has

given me back the will to live, and not in
the way you would suppose. Because of her
encouragement I am going now to offer marriage to her sister whom I adore."

For the first time Valentina saw her
husband look totally discomposed and she
didn't like it.

As the comte made to leave, the marquis caught his arm. "Jacques..."

"No, don't apologise to me. I am only
honoured at the notion but whilst I go to
see Sir Arthur Woodville, you should go on
your knees and beg your wife's pardon for
the slur on her honour. She is a jewel beyond
price." He bowed stiffly to Valentina. "Madame."

The door closed behind him with a snap
and the moment he had gone she turned
away, unable to face her husband.

"Valentina, I am most dreadfully sorry,"
he said the moment they were alone.

"He does not know the state of our relationship, otherwise he wouldn't have spoken of me to you as he did."

"That is of no account. I am quite aware
of your worth, and I had no right to believe
ill of either of you, but just seeing you
clasped in his arms as you were, was most

disconcerting. It was foolish of me to come to such a conclusion though."

"Please, don't apologise. It is quite understandable. We are all capable of making mistakes."

"And I have committed a grievous one. Perchance de Fontaine is correct and I am quite mad."

She sensed that he was close to her and she began to tremble, more so when he touched her arm.

"Allow me to make up for it in some way, Valentina," he begged.

She brushed away a tear which had spilled on to her cheek and then moved so he was not so close to her.

Taking a deep breath she answered, "You can do so by not mentioning the matter again."

His manner became withdrawn and he, too, stepped back to put more space between them.

"As you wish," he said curtly before striding out of the room and leaving her alone once more.

Thirteen

The bells of St. George's rang incessantly, filling the air around Hanover Square with the carillon. The square and the surrounding streets were choked with carriages as Daphne Woodville was married to Jacques Henri Phillipe de Fontaine.

The wedding was taking place almost exactly a year after Valentina's but the bride's radiance on this occasion hardly repeated her own. Valentina had never seen her sister so happy, nor the comte whom she had witnessed in his most wretched hour. She could not help shed a tear, which was quite natural except that she was crying, not out of emotion, but from self-pity.

At her side sat the marquis and to the world everything appeared as it should, but soon, she knew, the pretence would end once and for all.

After the bride and groom had been sent off on the first stage of their journey to the small country estate which was part of Daphne's dowry, the guests continued their merrymaking, and all those who saw Valentina had no notion she was not as happy as her sister that day.

Throughout the entire proceedings Lady Woodville looked flushed with happiness and confided in her elder daughter, "I did not hope to see Daphne so well settled."

"She deserves to be, Mama. She is a good, dutiful daughter, a devoted sister, and will make a wonderful wife."

"You both do. In all the excitement I have not heard you speak of your plans for the summer."

She started in alarm for it was the one thing she did not wish to discuss. "Daphne and Monsieur de Fontaine are joining us at Beechings," Lady Woodville went on a moment later, "after a month in their own place, naturally."

"Oh, Mama, may I come, too?" she asked.

"Naturally. It will be delightful to have both my married daughters and their husbands together at Beechings."

Valentina looked away. "Stockdale will be at his own estate. He has a deal of business there, I know."

Lady Woodville looked at her askance. "Then, surely, that is where you should be. You can both join us later when you are able."

Valentina was exasperated, but could say no more for the moment and she dreaded the time when she would have to break the news to her parents who would, quite rightly, blame her for the rift.

The celebration continued until late, which was, at least, a great diversion for her, and when she returned to Piccadilly with her husband and mother-in-law, the dowager yawned.

"What a very satisfactory day," she declared. "I am so glad to see Monsieur de Fontaine well settled after all his trials and your Mama must be quite relieved to have you both married."

The marquis toyed with the gold knob on the end of his stick as Valentina averted her eyes from the all seeing ones of her mother-in-law.

"She will have to see your brother settled now, and that is infinitely more difficult. He seems a trifle rackety."

"All young men of that age are a trifle wild," her son pointed out.

"I do not recall that you were," she said indignantly, and then to Valentina again, "it would be a tragedy if he were to choose wrongly. Alexander, *you* must take him to task."

He sighed, for it was clear to Valentina he had other matters on his mind and she could easily guess what they were.

"Yes, Mama."

She sailed into the candlelit hall of the house saying, "Good night, my children. I must soon make my departure for I have long overstayed my welcome here."

Valentina began to assure her it wasn't so but she did not heed it. Instead she said to her son, "You really are very remiss, my boy. Can you not see that your wife is looking quite hag ridden? I cannot conceive why you allow her to attend every function of the *ton*. It really is quite unnecessary. You must see to it that she rests far more than she does now."

He smiled faintly and kissed her cheek. "I will do that, Mama."

Valentina dutifully kissed her cheek, too, and bade her goodnight. She would have followed the dowager up the stairs, only the marquis said, "Valentina, we have some matters to discuss. Now that the wedding is over... Perhaps tomorrow..."

"Let us be done with it now," she suggested, weary, as her mother-in-law had noticed.

The marquis inclined his head. "As you wish. In the library or your sitting room?"

"There will be a fire in my sitting room. We will not be disturbed in there."

He followed her up the stairs, both of them still wearing their wedding finery. When he closed the door behind him Valentina went to the fire. Although it was far from cold outside she felt chilled deep in her bones.

"Mother is correct. You do look strained,

Valentina. This year has been an ordeal for you and you have borne it well."

"I am gratified to have pleased you."

"I own you have done very well and contrived to hide your true feelings." He paused to take a pinch of snuff before going on, "It's ironic that entirely due to your efforts we are now looked upon as unfashionably devoted."

Valentina allowed him to talk without answering, for she could not trust herself to speak.

"You will no doubt have been making plans for your future." He paused to allow her to comment and when she did not he drew an almost imperceptible sigh. "It is regrettable that Mayne has proved so inconstant a lover. I realise that must pain you, but no doubt there will be others anxious to replace him in your affections."

He paused yet again before going on, "This sad impasse in our lives is no fault of yours, Valentina. You made no pretence of your feelings from the outset so I will not hold you to blame, and you need harbour no fears for your future situation. I shall ensure that you have every comfort due to one of your position."

"Oh, do please stop!" she cried at last, unable to bear his magnanimity any longer.

"Of course, if that is what you wish. We shall discuss it another time when you are not so fatigued."

She turned to face him then. "No, we shall discuss it now and be done with it."

"As you please."

He took another pinch of snuff and Valentina watched him with scarce concealed resentment. "You talk a great deal of my plans for the future, but nothing of your own."

He drew a sigh. "I own that I have not given much thought to it."

She cast him a look of disbelief. "That seems exceeding odd to me."

"Of late I have been engaged in helping de Fontaine clarify his affairs."

"You have had a year to think about your future."

He fixed her with a steady stare. "A year ago I certainly had plans, but as you are aware they were thwarted. However, there is no advantage now in discussing that."

Valentina twisted her hands together in anguish. "Don't be a hypocrite! Do you think I'm just a green girl not to know you plan to marry Lady Goodhayes as soon as you are rid of me?"

His eyebrows rose a fraction, "My dear Valentina, I assure you it is not so. Lady Goodhayes and I are old friends and I hope always will be, but we are sadly unsuited to marriage."

Valentina was suddenly less certain of herself. "What of the child?"

"Toby? A pleasant boy from all I have observed."

"You speak with remarkable detachment about your own son."

He laughed then. "That is a ridiculous statement and quite untrue. Who could have told you that Banbury Tale I wonder? Sir Phineas was my greatest friend. I would not have cuckolded him even if Lady Goodhayes was not the most modest and loyal of wives."

Suddenly she recalled who had given her the so-called information. In her despair it had not occurred to her to disbelieve him.

"Sir Phineas...was ill for a twelve month before he died."

The marquis laughed again. "Not so ill, I assure you." He turned away to snuff a candle which was guttering dangerously in a candlestick. "It is a pity she and I are so unsuited; I must own she would make an excellent wife."

"I... would try to be an excellent wife," Valentina said breathlessly.

He wiped his hands carefully on his lawn handkerchief. "Oh, I dare say you will once you fulfil all those romantic notions of yours."

Suddenly she recalled the times before they were married, when a score of young men vied to win her affection with extravagant declarations. The marquis never attempted to overpower her with his attentions as so many of the others did, and yet he was always there, a hand to steady her when she climbed down from her carriage, an arm to take her into supper, and a compliment, perhaps not in such flowery words as others used, but sincere for all that. Now his cold disinterest hit her as strongly as a blow, and was as unbearable as physical abuse. She knew she deserved to be despised by him, but it was painful all the same.

The realisation of her own foolishness in throwing away a truer love than any of the others had come too late, something which caused the tears to well up in her eyes and to slide silently down her cheeks.

Aware that he was coming towards her, Valentina attempted to hide her tears by averting her face.

"I would have supposed you'd display a trifle more delight at the prospect of being free of me at last."

She turned her head away in shame. "How can I? My freedom means nothing to me any more. I only wish for a chance to make you happy, even though I know it is far too late."

She looked at him at last as the tears streamed down her cheeks, unchecked now. "You married a foolish empty-headed girl. I'm a woman now and I love you with all my heart."

The news seemed not to move him at all; he just continued to gaze at her. He was totally inscrutable, displaying neither pleasure nor scorn.

Once again she averted her eyes. Suddenly, unable to bear the silence any longer she gathered up her skirts and fled across the room.

"And I have never ceased to adore you," he said as she reached the door.

The room swayed unsteadily as she paused with her hand on the door knob.

Then, slowly, she turned, hardly daring to trust the evidence of her own ears. Then as she looked at him in amazement she realised at last that his own anxiety had been as great as hers.

An uncertain smile crossed her face and when he held out his arms she ran into them to be enveloped by his embrace. Held close against him she could scarcely breathe but Valentina had no intention of moving away for fear this should only be a dream.

When she looked up at him to ascertain it was not so, he kissed her gently on the lips as if savouring the moment for an eternity. Inevitably though, the kiss became more insistent and she responded instinctively, matching his passion with her own.

"I did doubt of late that this could ever happen," he whispered into her hair as she continued to cling on to him desperately. "Lady Goodhayes always doubted that it would, but I kept on hoping."

She looked up at him questioningly then. "Lady Goodhayes?"

"She is a good friend, Valentina, and would be to you if you permitted it. She had my confidence from the start, just as your sister had yours. Daphne would never betray that confidence, but some of the remarks she has unwittingly made gave me a little hope for our future."

"Why, if you love me, did you offer me my freedom?"

He smiled at her whilst caressing her hair and looking at her as if he had never seen her before.

"I am known to be a gambling man, and this is the greatest gamble I have ever made. With an independent spirit such as yours, my love, it would have been foolish of me to force you to my will. I hoped that by offering you your freedom the prospect of it would lose its attraction as time passed."

"And if it had not?"

"I would have kept my word to you, and lost the greatest prize of all."

She pressed close to him once more. "I am more ashamed than I can say. I could not see past all the glitter to the real gold beyond."

She looked up at him again. Her entire body trembled in the anticipation of his kiss and when it came she felt more alive than ever before.

"We shall become boring with our devotion," she said breathlessly at last.

"I adore you," he whispered against her lips before swinging her off her feet and into his arms. "There have been many occasions when I have been bound to curb the instinct to do this. My patience is at an end, madam."

She laughed delightedly and buried her head in his shoulder as he carried her towards the door.

"It shall be as you wish, my love, for I am and always will be your dutiful and devoted wife."